KT-196-248

BOOKS BY ELMORE LEONARD

ELMORE LEONARD

Hombre

HarperTorch
An Imprint of HarperCollinsPublishers

HARPERTORCH
An Imprint of HarperCollins*Publishers*
10 East 53rd Street
New York, New York 10022-5299

Copyright © 1961 by Elmore Leonard, Inc.
Front cover art by Tim Cox (*www.TimCox.com*)
Excerpt from *The Bounty Hunters* copyright © 1953 by Elmore Leonard, Inc.
ISBN: 0-380-82224-5

First HarperTorch paperback printing: March 2002

HarperCollins ®, HarperTorch™, and ♥™ are trademarks of Harper-Collins Publishers Inc.

Printed in the United States of America

Visit HarperTorch on the World Wide Web at www.harpercollins.com

10 9 8 7 6 5 4 3

At first I wasn't sure at all where to begin. When I asked advice, this man from the *Florence Enterprise* said begin at the beginning, the day the coach departed from Sweetmary with everybody aboard. Which sounded fine until I got to doing it. Then I saw it wasn't the beginning at all. There was too much to explain at one time. Who the people were, where they were going and all. Also, starting there didn't tell enough about John Russell.

He is the person this story is mainly about. If it had not been for him, we would all be dead and there wouldn't be anybody telling this. So I will begin with the first time I ever saw John Russell. I think you will see why after you learn a few things about him. Three weeks went by before I saw him again and that was the day the coach left Sweetmary. It was in the afternoon, right after they had brought the McLaren girl over from Fort Thomas.

Some things, especially concerning the McLaren girl and also some of my ideas about John Russell at the time, are embarrassing to put on paper. But I was advised to imagine I was telling it to a good friend and not worry about what other people might think. Which is what I have done. If there's anything anybody wants to skip, like innermost thoughts in places, just go ahead.

As for the title, it could be called any one of John Russell's names; he had more than one as you will see. But I think *Hombre*, which Henry Mendez and others called him sometimes and just means *man*, is maybe the best.

For the record, the day the coach left Sweetmary was Tuesday, August 12, 1884. Figure back three weeks if you want to know what day I first met John Russell. It was not at Sweetmary, but at Delgado's Station.

Carl Everett Allen
Contention, Arizona

1

Here is where I think it begins—with Mr. Henry Mendez, the Hatch & Hodges Division Manager at Sweetmary and still my boss at the time, asking me to ride the sixteen miles down to Delgado's with him in the mud wagon. I suspected the trip had to do with the company shutting down this section of the stage line; Mr. Mendez would see Delgado about closing his station and take an inventory of company property. But that was only part of the reason.

It turned out I was the one had to take the inventory. Mr. Mendez had something else on his mind. As soon as we got to the station, he sent one of Delgado's boys out to John Russell's place to get him.

Until that day John Russell was just a name I had written in the Division account book a few times during the past year. So many dollars paid to John Russell for so many stage horses. He was a mustanger. He would chase down green horses and harness-break them; then Mr. Mendez would buy what he wanted, and Russell and two White

Mountain Apaches who rode for him would deliver the horses to Delgado's or one of the other relay stations on the way south to Benson.

Mr. Mendez had bought maybe twenty-five or thirty from him during the past year. Now, I suspected, he wanted to tell Russell not to bring in any more since we were shutting down. I asked Mr. Mendez if that was so. He said no, he had already done that. This was about something else.

Like it was a secret. That was the trouble with Mr. Mendez when I worked for him. From a distance you could never tell he was Mexican. He never dressed like one, everything white like their clothes were made out of bedsheets. He didn't usually act like one. Except that his face, with those tobacco-stained looking eyes and drooping mustache, was always the same and you never knew what he was thinking. When he looked at you, it was like he knew something he wasn't telling, or was laughing at you, no matter what it was he said. That's when you could tell Henry Mendez was Mexican. He wasn't old. Not fifty anyway.

Delgado's boy got back while we were having some coffee and said Russell would be here. A little while later we heard horses, so we went outside.

As we stood there seeing these three riders coming toward the adobe with the dust rising behind them, Mr. Mendez said to me, "Take a good look at Russell. You will never see another one like him as long as you live."

I will swear to the truth of that right now. Though it was not just his appearance.

The three riders came on, but giving the feeling that they were holding back some, not anxious to ride right up until they made sure everything was keno. When Russell pulled up, the two White Mountain Apaches with him slowed to a walk and came up on either side of him. Not close, out a ways, as if giving themselves room to move around in. All three of them were armed; I mean *armed*, with revolvers, with cartridge belts over their shoulder and carbines, which looked like Springfields at first.

As he sat there, that's when I got my first real look at John Russell.

Picture the belt down across his chest with the sun glinting on the bullets that filled most of the loops. Picture a stained, dirty looking straight-brim hat worn almost Indian-fashion, that is, uncreased and not cocked to either side, except his brim was curled some and there was a little dent down the crown.

Picture his face half shadowed by the hat. First you just saw how dark it was. Dark as his arms with the sleeves rolled above his elbows. Dark—I swear—as the faces of the two White Mountain boys. Then you saw how long his hair was, almost covering his ears, and how clean-shaved looking his face was. Right then you suspected he was more to those Apaches than a friend or a boss. I mean he could be a blood relation, no matter what his name was, and nobody in the world would bet he wasn't.

When Mr. Mendez spoke to him you believed it all the more. He stepped closer to John Russell's roan horse, and I remember the first thing he said.

He said, *"Hombre."*

Russell didn't say anything. He just looked at Mr. Mendez, though you couldn't see his eyes in the shadow of his hat brim.

"Which name today?" Mr. Mendez said. "Which do you want?"

Russell answered Mr. Mendez in Spanish then, just a few words, and Mr. Mendez said, in English, "We use John Russell. No symbol names. No Apache names. All right?" When Russell just nodded, Mr. Mendez said, "I was wondering what you decided. You said you would come to Sweetmary in two days."

Russell used Spanish again, more this time, evidently explaining something.

"Maybe it would look different to you if you thought about it in English," Mr. Mendez said and watched him closely. "Or if you spoke about it now in English."

"It's the same," Russell said, all of a sudden in English. In good English that had only a speck of accent, just a faint edge that you would wonder every time you heard him if it really was some kind of accent.

"But it's a big something to think about," Mr. Mendez said. "Going to Contention. Going there to live among white men. To live as a white man on land a white man has given you. To have to speak English to people no matter what language you think in."

"There it is," Russell said. "I'm still thinking all the different ways."

"Sure," Mr. Mendez said. "You could sell the land. Buy a horse and a new gun with some of the money. Give the rest to the hungry ones at the San Carlos Indian agency. Then you got nothing."

Russell shrugged. "Maybe so."

"Or you sell only the herd and grow corn on the land and make *tizwin*, enough to keep you drunk for seven years."

"Even that," Russell said.

"Or you can work the herd and watch it grow," Mr. Mendez said. "You can marry and raise a family. You can live there the rest of your life." He waited a little. "You want some more ways to picture it?"

"I have too many ways now," Russell said. But he didn't sound worried about it.

That didn't satisfy Mr. Mendez. He was trying to convince him of something and kept at it. He said then, "I hear it's a good house."

Russell nodded. "If living there is worth it to you."

"Man," Mendez said, like something good was staring at Russell and he didn't know enough to take it. "What do you want?"

Russell looked down at him. In that unhurried easy way he said, "Maybe a *mescal* if there's some inside, uh?"

Delgado laughed and said something in Spanish. Mr. Mendez shrugged and both of them turned to the adobe.

I was watching Russell though. He dismounted, still holding his carbine, which I now saw was an old .56-56 Spencer, and came right toward me looking at the ground, then looking up quick as he must have sensed me. For a second we were close and I saw his eyes. They had that same tell-nothing-but-know-everything expression as Henry Mendez's eyes. That same Mexican, Indian look. Only John Russell's eyes were blue, light-blue looking in his Indian-dark face. Maybe that doesn't sound like anything, but I'll tell you it gave me the strangest feeling.

The two Apaches carried Springfields, as I had guessed. They held them cradled across one arm and even with the bullet belts and all, they looked kind of funny. Mainly because of their vests and straw hats that were very narrow and turned up all around. They went inside too and I followed.

Only I didn't stay long. Mr. Mendez sent me out to the equipment shed to start the inventory. Then over to see about the feed stores. So it was maybe a half hour before I got back to the main adobe. Five saddle horses along with the mud wagon were standing in front now instead of three.

Inside, I saw Mr. Mendez and John Russell at one end of the long table the stage passengers sat at. Russell's carbine lay on the table, like he never went far without it; another thing that was just like an Apache.

At the bar along the right wall stood his two Apache riders. Down from them were two more men. I didn't look at them good till I sat down next to Mr. Mendez. Right away then I got the feeling something was going on. It was too quiet. Mendez was looking over at the bar; Russell down at his drink, as if thinking or listening.

So I looked at the two men again. I recognized them as hands who rode for a Mr. Wolgast who supplied beef to the reservation up at San Carlos. I would see them in Sweetmary every once in a while and they would most always be drunk. But it was a minute or two before I remembered their names. One was Lamarr Dean, who was about my age, maybe a year older. The other one's name was

Early; he was said to have served time at Yuma Prison.

Delgado poured them a whisky like he'd rather be doing something else. Early, who wore his hat funneled down over his eyes and ordinarily didn't talk much, said, "I guess anybody can come in here."

"If they allow Indians," this Lamarr Dean said. He was looking at the two Apaches. They heard him, you could tell, but didn't pay any attention. Of course not, I realized; they didn't know any English.

The one named Early asked Delgado, "When did they start letting Indians drink?" I didn't hear what Delgado answered.

Lamarr Dean stood with his side against the bar so that he was facing the first Apache. "Maybe they have been drinking *tizwin*," he said. "Maybe that's where they bought the nerve to come in here."

Early said, "It would take a week with *tizwin*."

"They got time," Dean said. "What else do they do?"

"That's *mescal*," Early said then.

Lamarr Dean went on staring. "I guess," he said. He moved toward the first Apache, holding his drink, his elbow sliding along the edge of the bar until he was right next to the Apache. Early stayed where he was.

"*Mescal*," Lamarr Dean said. "But it's still not allowed. Not even sticky-sweet Mex drinks."

The first Apache, not even knowing what was going on, raised his glass. It was right up to his mouth when Lamarr Dean nudged him, reaching out and pushing him a little, and the *mescal* spilled over the Apache's chin and down the front of his vest. He looked at Lamarr Dean then, not understanding, I guess not sure if it was an accident or what.

"They just can't hold it," Lamarr Dean said. "Nobody knows why, but it's a fact of nature." He raised his whisky right in front of the Apache, as if daring the Apache to try the same thing on him.

That was when Russell stood up. His eyes never left Lamarr Dean, but his right hand closed on the Spencer and it was down at his side as he walked over the few steps to the bar.

Lamarr Dean was facing the Apache, starting to drink, sipping at the whisky to give the Apache all the chance he needed. Like saying come on, nudge my arm and see what happens. Then his chin raised as he started to down the whisky.

Russell was right there. But he didn't nudge him. He didn't ask or tell him to leave the Apache alone. Or say anything like, "If you want to pick on somebody, try me." He didn't give Lamarr a chance to know he was there.

He just swung the barrel of the Spencer up clean

and quick and before you had a chance to believe it was happening the barrel shattered the glass right against Lamarr Dean's mouth. Lamarr jumped back, dropping the broken pieces and with blood all over his hand and face.

I think he would have tore into Russell the next second, with his fists or his revolver, but now the Spencer was leveled at his belly, almost touching it. Early had his hand on his gun, but it had happened so fast even he couldn't do anything.

Russell said, "No more, uh?"

Lamarr Dean didn't say anything. I don't think he could talk.

Russell said, "Before you leave, put money down for a *mescal*."

That was John Russell, no older than I was at twenty-one and no more Apache than I was. Except he had lived with them—the wild free ones in the mountains and the wild caught ones up at San Carlos—about half his life and that made the difference. He was perhaps one-part Mexican, according to Mr. Mendez, and three-parts white. But I will go into more of that a little later. Right here I just wanted to tell about the first time I ever saw him.

Now, three weeks later, here is where I was advised to begin—with them bringing the McLaren girl over from Fort Thomas in an ambulance wagon and the lieutenant taking her right into the Alamosa Hotel.

I was out in front of the Hatch & Hodges office at the time, directly across the street, and I got a clear look at the girl even with all the people around. She was seventeen or eighteen and certainly pretty. Though maybe pretty wasn't the word, the way her hair was cut almost as short as a boy's and her face dark from the sun. But she looked good anyway. Even after living with Apaches over a month and after all the things they must have done to her.

Somebody said the girl had been taken by Chiricahuas on a raid and held four or five weeks before a patrol out of Fort Thomas surprised their *ranchería* and found her. She had stayed at Thomas a while and now this officer was to put her on a stage for home. Some place around St. David.

Only by now there weren't any more southbound stages, and there hadn't been for over a week. There were notices all over, but that was like the Army to bring her all the way over to Sweetmary not knowing Hatch & Hodges had shut down its stage service. They told the lieutenant over at the hotel, but he wanted to hear it directly from the company. So he sent one of the escort soldiers for Henry Mendez who went right over.

I stayed out front hoping to get another look at

the girl if she came out. That's why I was still there when John Russell appeared, which was some fifteen minutes later.

Somebody might laugh, but just for something to do I was picturing the McLaren girl and I sitting alone in the hotel café. We were talking and I heard myself say, "It must have been a very terrible experience, being with those Apaches." Her eyes stayed on her coffee, and she didn't say anything to that.

So we talked about other things. I heard myself speaking calmly in a low tone, telling her how I would be looking into some other business now that this office was closing. Go some place else. With no family here there was nothing to keep me. Then I pictured us traveling together. (Do you see how one thing led to another?) But what would we travel in?

That's when I thought of the mud wagon, the light spring coach Mr. Mendez and I had taken to Delgado's that day. It was still here.

I said to the McLaren girl, "Since you're anxious to leave and there's no regular stage, I wonder if you would like to ride along with me?" (Which proves that using the mud wagon was my idea; whether Mr. Mendez agrees or not.)

Then I skipped the part where she says yes and goes and gets her things and all and pictured the two of us in the coach again. It was night and we were traveling south. Above the wind and the rattle sounds I'd hear her start to cry and put my arm around her and lift her chin and say something that would calm her. She'd sniffle and nestle closer, and even with the peculiar haircut I'd know she wasn't any boy.

We might have rode along in that coach the whole night while I just stood there in front of the office. But both the McLaren girl and the coach disappeared the second I saw John Russell. The new John Russell.

He was sitting his roan horse on this side of the street but down a ways. He was watching the hotel, sitting there like he'd always been there. Smoking a cigarette, I remember that too. But the only thing I recognized about him right away was his hat, worn straight and the brim just curled a little.

Now he had on a suit. It was a pretty worn dark gray one, but it fit him all right. You could see that his hair had been cut. Without the hair covering the ears and that shell belt and all he wasn't someone you would stare at. At least not till you saw him close.

That was not till a few minutes later. Until Mr. Mendez came out of the hotel and Russell nudged his roan up to in front of the office. As he dismounted he looked at me over the saddle and there was that tell-nothing expression, looking at me no different than the way he had looked at Lamarr

Dean the moment before he broke a whisky glass against his mouth.

Mr. Mendez was standing there now. He said, "You're going to do it?"

"I'm going there to sell the place," Russell said.

Mr. Mendez seemed to stare at him for awhile, thinking or just looking, I don't know which. Finally he said, "It's up to you. You can be white or Mexican or Indian. But now it pays you to be a white man. To look like a white man for awhile. When you go to Contention, you say, How are you? I'm John Russell. I own the Russell place. Some people will remember you from before; some won't. But they will all know you as John Russell who owns the Russell place. You look at it. If you don't like it, sell it. If you like it, keep it, and see what happens and then decide." Mr. Mendez almost seemed to smile. "Did you know life was that simple?"

"I've learned some things," John Russell said. "That's why I sell it."

He left his roan horse in front and went with Mr. Mendez back across the street to the Alamosa Hotel. Mr. Mendez hadn't bothered to introduce us. In fact he had not bothered to look at me at all. Which was all right.

A little later this Mexican boy who worked for us took Russell's horse around to the stable. I was in the office then, having given up on seeing the

McLaren girl again. The boy came in through the back carrying Russell's blanket roll and carbine and put them down on the passenger bench. I remember thinking, What will he do without the Spencer if Lamarr Dean or Early are over there at the Alamosa?

I also remember thinking at the time that dressing like a white man and taking a white man's name wasn't ever going to hide the Apache in him. I don't mean Apache blood. I just mean after the way he had lived, how was he even going to convince anybody he was a white man? He didn't even prefer to speak English. It was things like that gave you the feeling he had no use for white men or our ways.

According to Mr. Mendez he was most likely three-parts white, as I have said, and the rest Mexican on his mother's side. John Russell himself had no memory of his father and only some memory of living in a Mexican village. Probably in Sonora. At that time they say the Apaches were forever raiding the little pueblos and carrying off whatever they needed, clothes, weapons, some women, and sometimes boys young enough to be brought up Apache-style. Which is what must have happened to John Russell. Piecing things together, he must have lived with them about from the time he was six to about age twelve.

Here is where a James Russell, late of Con-

tention, comes in. At that time he owned supply
wagons contracted to the Army, and he was at Fort
Thomas when this boy who was called *Ish-kay-
nay* was brought in with some prisoners. The boy
was assigned to a work detail under James Russell
and that was how the two became friends. Just a
month later, when James Russell sold his business
and went to settle in Contention, he took the boy
with him and gave him his American name, John
Russell. Five years or so passed and the boy even
went to school there. Then all of a sudden he left
and went up to San Carlos and joined the reservation police as if to become Apache again. (Here
they called him *Tres Hombres*, which I will try to
tell you about later.)

Now we are almost up to the present. He was
with the police about three years, mostly up at
Turkey Creek and Whiteriver. Then he moved
again. Off on his own now as a mustanger. (I guess
to break horses you don't have to be halter-broke
yourself, because he was pretty good at it Mr.
Mendez said.)

A month ago, then, when Mr. James Russell
died, the word was passed to John Russell through
Mr. Mendez that he had been left Russell's place
outside Contention. Mr. Mendez wanted to put
him on a coach and send him down there in style,
but Russell kept backing off. Finally, when he did

show up willing, there were no more stagecoaches. As I have explained.

Hatch & Hodges was leaving Sweetmary partly because there wasn't enough business from here south; partly because the railroad was taking too much business other places. But that day, all of a sudden, you'd never know we were hard up for business.

First the McLaren girl had come. Then John Russell. Then, right after he and Mr. Mendez left, a mustered-out soldier from Thomas came in looking for passage to Bisbee. He was going to get married in a week and anxious to get there. I told him how it was and he left, walking over to the hotel.

It wasn't long after that Dr. Favor came.

I had never seen him before, but I had heard of him. So when he came in and introduced himself, I knew this was Dr. Alexander Favor, the Indian Agent at San Carlos.

His name was heard because San Carlos was so close, but not too much. You heard of Indian Agents if they were very good, like John Clum, or if they were bad and got caught dealing poorly with the Indians for their own personal gain. You heard when they weren't at the reservation anymore and you heard of the new man arriving. So I didn't know much about Dr. Favor. Only that he had been up at San Carlos about two years and had a wife that was supposed to be very pretty and about fifteen years younger than he was.

He came in so unexpectedly I probably acted dumb at first. He stood with his hands and his hat on the counter which separated the waiting room from the office part, looking straight at me and never away. He was a big man, not so tall but heavy, with kind of reddish-brown hair—what there was of it—and a finely-kept half-moon beard on his chin. But no mustache. You have probably seen the style I am talking about.

He knew the stage line had stopped running. But what about hiring a rig and driver? I told him we were out of business, even for hiring. He said, but what was the possibility? We talked about that for a while and that was when I got the idea of using the mud wagon. Not just for him but for the McLaren girl too, and just like before I could see myself sitting in it with her.

That's when I started to get excited about the idea. I wanted to get away from here. Why not in the mud wagon? I could talk to Dr. Favor on the way to Bisbee, which was where he wanted to go, and ask his advice about what business to get into. A man like Dr. Favor would know, and maybe he would even have some good connections. Between that and the idea of seeing the McLaren girl, it sounded better and better and finally I got the

Mexican boy, who was out front again, and sent him after Mr. Mendez.

About fifteen minutes passed. Dr. Favor came through the gate at the end of the counter and sat at Mr. Mendez's desk. We didn't talk much and I felt dumb again. Finally Mr. Mendez came in.

He came right through the gate. I introduced them and Mr. Mendez nodded. Dr. Favor didn't rise or even reach out his hand.

He said, "We're talking about hiring a coach."

Mr. Mendez looked at me. "Didn't Carl tell you? This office is closed."

"But you still have a coach here," Dr. Favor said. "He called it a mud wagon."

"That." Mr. Mendez leaned back against the counter. "We move our office records in it when we leave."

"Come back to get them," Dr. Favor said.

I said, "They have to be in Bisbee Friday." That was in three days. I even added, "If they don't get there, it'll be too late."

Mr. Mendez just shrugged. "If I could do something—"

I said, "Why not use the mud wagon and come back? We could do that without any trouble."

Mr. Mendez was probably already mad because I was talking up, but he still looked patient. He said, "And who would drive it?"

"I could do it," I said. Which just came to me that moment.

"Do you think the company would put an inexperienced driver on a run like that?"

"Well," I said, "how do you get experience?"

"All of a sudden you want to be a driver."

"I'm trying to help Dr. Favor. If he has to be in Bisbee, I think the company should see he gets there."

"Within the company's power," Mr. Mendez said, still patient. "I think you and I can discuss this another time, uh?"

"That doesn't help Dr. Favor any."

Dr. Favor said, "What if I'm willing to let him drive?"

"You might also be willing to bring suit if something happens," Mr. Mendez said.

"If I bought the rig?" Dr. Favor said.

But Mr. Mendez shook his head. "It's not mine to sell."

"Then if I paid more than just our fares."

"You're anxious to get there," Mr. Mendez said.

"I thought you understood that."

Mr. Mendez nodded his head to the side. "Isn't that your buggy by the hotel? Use that."

"It's government property," Dr. Favor said. "There's a regulation about using it for private matters."

"We have regulations too."

"How much do you want?" Dr. Favor seemed just as patient as Mr. Mendez.

"Well, if there was a driver here."

"Then it comes down to a driver."

"And horses. We would have to get four, six horses."

"All right, get them."

"But I couldn't take responsibility for them," Mr. Mendez said. "Now there are no change stations working. The same horses would have to go all the way." Mr. Mendez shrugged. "If they don't make it, who pays for them?"

"I buy the horses," Dr. Favor said.

Mr. Mendez started to nod, very slowly, as if he was just understanding something. "You want to get there pretty bad, uh?"

"I have a feeling," Dr. Favor said, "you're going to find a driver." He pushed up out of the chair, his eyes on Mr. Mendez. "If I went over to the hotel now and had supper, that would give you about an hour to find a man and get ready. Say six-thirty."

"Tonight?"

"Why not?"

"I'll see," Mr. Mendez said.

"Do that," Dr. Favor said. He moved through the gate, taking his hat from the counter.

"But I won't promise you," Mr. Mendez said after him. The Indian agent just walked out, like it was settled.

I said, soon as he was gone, "Mr. Mendez, I know I can drive it."

"Driving a stage isn't something you know you can do," Mr. Mendez said.

"I've pulled the teams around from the yard plenty of times. And that mud wagon's lighter than a Concord."

"The horses pull it," he said. "Not you."

We argued some more, and finally I said, "Well, who else do you have?"

"Don't worry about it," he said.

"Well, I am worrying, because I want to go too."

He looked at me closely with those brown-stained eyes not telling anything, and I hoped my face was just as calm and natural.

"To talk to this Favor, uh? Get to know him?"

"Why not?"

"It's all right, Carl."

"I was thinking of some others too," I said. "An ex-soldier who was in here. And there's the McLaren girl."

Mr. Mendez nodded again as if he was thinking. "The McLaren girl. Sure," he said. "And maybe John Russell."

It was all right with me. "That would be five inside," I said.

"Six," Mr. Mendez said.

"Not if I'm driving."

Mr. Mendez shook his head. "You're inside like a passenger. How does that sound?"

"Well," I said, "could I ask who's going to drive it then?"

"I am," Mr. Mendez said. "Who else?"

The way Mr. Mendez decided to go all of a sudden didn't make any sense at all until I thought about it a while. And then I realized it might not have been so all of a sudden at that. He could have seen money in this right off and been leading Dr. Favor on, seeing to make about a month's wages in three days if he kept all the fares; and why wouldn't he? That was one thing.

The other was John Russell being here. I think Mr. Mendez wanted to get him on his way before he had time to change his mind; before he spent another night staring at the ceiling and counting all the reasons why he shouldn't go to Contention. Put him in a coach now and by morning Russell might be used to being close to white people again. But why Mr. Mendez bothered or cared was something else. Maybe because he was Mexican and John Russell was part Mexican. Does that make sense?

There was a lot to do before six-thirty. I had the Mexican boy get his father; they'd take care of the coach and horses. Mr. Mendez said he would go to the hotel for John Russell and the McLaren girl and also try and find the ex-soldier. So he would see me later.

Before he went though I reminded him I was going too, and he paid me my last wages. From then on I was no longer with Hatch & Hodges. It was a pretty good feeling, even not knowing what I was going to do in life now.

First thing, I went to the boarding house where I lived and put on my suit. It was pretty old and too small now, making me look skinnier than I was, but it would be all right for the trip. I didn't want to buy a new one in Sweetmary. I thought about buying a gun, but decided against that too; I'd be out of money before I left. I wrote to my mother who lived up at Manzanita with her sister, Mrs. R. V. Hungerford, telling her how I was leaving my position and would write again when I had found some place I liked. Then I rolled up my things in a blanket and went out and had something to eat. By the time I got back to the office it was almost six-thirty.

John Russell was waiting. He was sitting on the bench along the wall on the left. His blanket roll, with the cartridge belt wrapped around it and the Spencer inside with part of the barrel and stock showing, was next to him.

I'll admit he gave me a start, because it was dim in the office and I didn't expect to see anybody. I left my blanket roll by the door and went around behind the counter and started making out a passenger list and tickets. Might as well do it right, I thought. Then it started to feel funny, just the two of us there and nobody talking.

So I said, "You ready for your stagecoach ride?" His eyes raised and he nodded. That was all.

"What about your horse?"

"Henry Mendez bought it."

"How much he give you?"

"Ask him," Russell said.

"I just wondered, that's all."

"Ask him," Russell said again.

Why bother? I thought, and went on making out the list. I put all the names down but the ex-soldier's because I didn't know his. I just put down Ex-Soldier and never did change it, even when he came in a couple of minutes later with this canvas bag on his shoulder. He swung it down, bouncing it off the counter, and reached into his coat pocket.

"What's the fare?"

"I guess you saw Mendez," I said, and told him how much.

"I don't know the whyfor," he said. "But I'm for it."

He waited while I tore off one of the orange-colored tickets, then another one. "If any stops are open on the way, show this for meals. Drinks are extra. You hand it in when you reach your destination. The other one's for him." I nodded to Russell. "You want to hand it to him?"

The ex-soldier looked at the ticket as he walked over to the bench. He was a heavy man and his coat was tight-smooth across the back. I would judge him to have been about thirty-seven or -eight. "I see you're going to Contention," he said, handing the ticket to Russell. "I change there for Bisbee. Yesterday I was in the Army. Next week I'm a mining man and the week after I'll have a wife, one already arranged for and waiting. What do you think of that?"

John Russell pulled the blanket roll toward him as the man sat down, propping his feet on his canvas bag. "You saving your lamp oil?" the ex-soldier said to me.

"I guess we can spare some." I came around and put a match to the Rochester lamp that hung from the ceiling. Just then I heard the coach and I said, "Here it comes, boys."

You could hear the jingling, rattling sound coming from the equipment yard next door. Then through the window you could see it—smaller than a Concord and almost completely open with its canvas side-curtains rolled up and fastened—just turning out of the yard, and the next moment the jingling, rattling sound was right out front. Four horses were pulling the mud wagon; two spares were on twenty-foot lines tied to the back end.

The ex-soldier said, "I wouldn't complain if it was an ore wagon all loaded."

"It's mainly just for rainy spells," I explained. "Sometimes a heavy Concord gets mired down; but three teams can pull a mud wagon through about anything."

The Mexican boy and his father were both up on the boot. Then Mendez, who must have just crossed the street, was standing there. "Everybody's going," he said. Then looked at John Russell. "Your saddle is on the coach. Now I go up and get myself ready."

I waited till we heard him on the stairs, then told them how I had offered to drive this run, but now that I was a passenger it would be against the rules. "There's rules about who can ride up with the driver," I said, looking at John Russell and wondering if he had any ideas. But that was all the farther I got.

The man who came in was wearing range clothes and carrying a saddle which he let go of just inside the door and came on, looking straight at me, but not smiling like he was ready to say something friendly.

He was tall by the time he reached the counter, with that thin, stringy look of a rider and the *ching-ching* sound of spurs. Even the dust and horse-smell seemed to be still with him, and he reminded you of Lamarr Dean and Early and almost every one of them you ever saw: all made of the same leather and hardly ever smiling unless they were with their own look-alike brothers. Then they were always loud, loud talking and loud laughing. This one had a .44 Colt on his hip and his hat tipped forward with the brim curled almost to a point, the hat loose on his head but seeming to be part of him.

"Frank Braden," he said. His hands spread out along the edge of the counter.

I said, "Yessir?" as if I still worked for Hatch & Hodges.

"Write it down for that coach out front."

"That's a special run."

"I heard. That's why I'm going on it."

I looked down at the four orange cards on the counter, lining them up evenly. "I'm afraid that one's full-up. Four here and those two. That is all the coach holds."

"You can get another on," he said. Telling me, not asking.

"Well, I don't see how."

"On top."

"No one's allowed to ride with the driver. That's a company rule. I was just telling these boys here, certain people can ride inside, certain people outside."

"You say they're going?" He nodded toward the bench.

"Yessir. Both of them."

He turned without another word and walked over to John Russell with that soft *ching*-ing spur sound.

He said, "That boy at the counter said you got a stage ticket."

John Russell opened his hand on his lap. "This?"

"That's it. You give it to me and you can take the next stage."

"I have to take this one," Russell said.

"No, you want to is all. But it would be better if you waited. You can get drunk tonight. How does that sound?"

"I have to take this one," John Russell said. "I have to take it and I want to take it."

"Leave him alone," the ex-soldier said then. "You come late, you find your own way."

Frank Braden looked at him. "What did you say?"

"I said why don't you leave him alone." His tone changed. All of a sudden it sounded friendlier, more reasonable. "He wants to take this stage, let him take it," the ex-soldier said.

You heard that *ching* sound again as Frank Braden shifted around to face the ex-soldier. He stared at him and said, "I guess I'll use your ticket instead."

The ex-soldier hadn't moved, his big hands resting on his knees, his feet still propped on the canvas bag. "You just walk in," he said, "and take somebody else's seat?"

Braden's pointed hat brim moved up and down. "That's the way it is."

The ex-soldier glanced at John Russell, then over at me. "Somebody's pulling a joke on somebody," he said.

Russell didn't say anything. He had made a cigarette and now he lit it, looking at Braden as he blew the smoke up in the air.

"You think I come in here to kid?" Braden asked the ex-soldier.

"Look here, this boy is going to Contention," the ex-soldier explained, "and I'm going to Bisbee to get married after twelve years of Army. We got places to go and no reason to give up our seats."

"All this *we*," Braden said. "I'm talking to you."

The ex-soldier didn't know what to say. And, even with his size, he didn't know what to do with Braden standing over him and not giving an inch. He glanced at John Russell again, then over to me like he'd thought of something. "What kind of a business you run?" he said. "You let a man walk in here and say he's taking your seat—after paying your fare and all—and the company doesn't do a thing about it?"

"Maybe I better get Mr. Mendez," I said. "He's upstairs."

"I think he ought to know about this," the ex-soldier said and started to rise. Braden stepped in closer and the ex-soldier looked up, almost straight up, and you could see then that he was afraid but trying hard not to show it.

"This is our business," Braden said. "You don't want somebody else's nose stuck in."

The ex-soldier seemed to get his nerve back—I guess because he realized he had to do something—and he said, "We better settle this right now."

Braden didn't budge. He said, "Are you wearing a gun?"

"Now wait a minute."

"If you aren't," Braden said, "you better get one."

"You can't just threaten a man like that," the ex-soldier said. "There are witnesses here seeing you threaten me."

Braden shook his head. "No, they heard you call me a dirty name."

"I never called you anything."

"Even if they didn't hear it," Braden said, "I did."

"I never said a word!"

"I'm going to walk out on the street," Braden said. "If you don't come out inside a minute, I'll have to come back in."

That's all there was to it. The ex-soldier stared

up at Braden, the cords in his neck standing out, his hands spread and clamped on his knees. And even as he gave up, as he let himself lean back against the wall, he was holding on, knowing he had backed down and it was over, but doing it gradually so we wouldn't see the change come over him. Braden held out his hand. The ex-soldier gave him his ticket. Then he picked up his bag and walked out.

Braden didn't even offer to pay him for the ticket. He watched the ex-soldier till he was gone, then walked over to his saddle and carried it out to the coach. I could feel him right outside, but it bothered me that I hadn't done anything. Or Russell hadn't. I motioned him over to the counter and he came, taking his time and stepping out his cigarette.

"Listen," I said, "shouldn't we have done something?"

"It wasn't my business," Russell said.

"But what if he had taken your ticket?" I stared at him and this close you could see that he was young. His face was thin and you saw those strange blue-colored eyes set in the darkness of his skin.

Russell said, "You would have to be sure he was making it something to kill over."

"He made it plain enough," I said.

"If you were sure," Russell said, "and if the

ticket was worth it to you, then you'd do something to keep it."

"But I don't think that soldier even had a gun."

Russell said, "That's up to him if he doesn't carry one." Even the way he said it made me mad; so calm about it.

"He would have helped you and you know it," I said.

"I don't know it," Russell said. "If he did, it would be up to him. But it wouldn't be any of his business."

Just like that. He walked back to the bench and just then Mendez came in. Now he was wearing a coat and hat and carrying a maleta bag and a sawed-off shotgun.

"Time," Mendez said, sounding almost happy about it. He came through the gate to get something from his desk. That gave me the chance to tell what Braden had done, sounding disgusted as I told it so Mendez would have no doubt what I thought about Braden's trick.

"Then we still have six," Mendez said. That was all.

And that was the six—seven counting Mendez—who left Sweetmary that Tuesday, August 12.

Nothing much happened just before we left. Russell asked to ride up with Mendez, saying they could talk about things.

"Talk," Mendez said. "You can't hear yourself."

He pushed Russell toward the coach. "Go on. See what it's like."

Then there was a talk between Mendez and Dr. Favor. Probably about all the other people in what was supposed to be a hired coach. I heard Mendez say, "I haven't seen any money yet." They talked a while and finally must have settled it.

The seating inside was as follows: Russell, the McLaren girl, and I riding backwards, across from Braden, Mrs. Favor, and Dr. Favor. Which was perfect. We sat there a while, almost dark inside after Mendez dropped the side curtains, not saying anything, feeling the coach move up and down on its leather thorough braces as the boy who worked for us put the traveling bags in the rear end boot and covered them with a canvas.

I tried to think of something to say to the McLaren girl, hardly believing she was next to me. But I decided to wait a while before speaking. Let her get comfortable and used to everybody.

So I just started picturing her. She was too close to look right at. But I could feel her there. You had the feeling, when you pictured her, that she looked like a boy more than a woman. Not her face. It was a girl's face with a girl's eyes. It was her body and the way she moved; the thinness of her body and the way she had walked up the hotel steps. You had the feeling she would run and swim. I could almost see her come out of the wa-

ter with her short hair glistening wet and pressed
to her forehead. I could see her smiling too, for
some reason.

Mrs. Favor was watching the McLaren girl,
staring right at her, so I had a chance to look at
Mrs. Favor. Audra was her name, and she was nice
looking all right: thin, but still very womanly looking, if you understand me. That was the thing
about her. If anybody ever says *woman* to me, like
"You should have seen that woman," or, "Now
there was a woman for you," I would think of Audra Favor, thinking of her as Audra, too, not as
Mrs. Favor, the Indian Agent's wife.

That was because one got the feeling she was
not with her husband. Dr. Favor was older than
she was, at least fifteen years older, which put her
about thirty, and he could have been just another
man sitting there. That would be something to
watch, I decided. To see if she paid any attention
to him.

Frank Braden, I noticed, looked right at Mrs.
Favor. With his head turned his face was close to
hers and he stared right at her, maybe thinking nobody could see him in the dimness, or maybe not
caring if they did.

Just before we left, I raised up to straighten my
coat and sneaked a look at the McLaren girl. Her
eyes were lowered, not closed, but looking down
at her hands. Russell, his hat tilted forward a little,

was looking at his hands too. They were folded on his lap.

What would these people think, I wondered, if they knew he'd been living like an Apache most of his life, right up until a little while ago? Would it make a difference to them? I had a feeling it would. I didn't think of myself as one of them, then; now I don't see why I should have left myself out. To tell the truth, I wasn't at all pleased about Russell sitting in the same coach with us.

When the coach started to roll I said, "Well, I guess we'll be together for a while."

2

There wasn't much talking at all until Mrs. Favor started after the McLaren girl. I saw her watching the girl for the longest time and finally she said, "Are those Indian beads?"

The McLaren girl looked up. "It's a rosary."

"I don't know why I thought they were Indian beads," Mrs. Favor said. Her voice soft and sort of lazy sounding, the kind of voice that most of the time you aren't sure if the person is kidding or being serious.

"You might say they are Indian beads," the girl said. "I made them."

"During your experience?"

Dr. Favor said, "Audra," very low, meaning for her to keep quiet.

"I hope I didn't remind you of something unpleasant," Mrs. Favor said.

Braden, I noticed, was looking at the McLaren girl too. "What happened?" he said.

The McLaren girl did not answer right away,

and Mrs. Favor leaned toward the girl. "If you don't want to talk about it, I can understand."

"I don't mind," the McLaren girl said.

Braden was still looking at her. He said again, "What happened?"

"I thought everybody knew," the McLaren girl said.

"Well," Braden said. "I guess I've been away."

"She was taken by Apaches," Mrs. Favor said. "With them, how long, a month?"

The McLaren girl nodded. "It seemed longer."

"I can imagine," Mrs. Favor said. "Did they treat you all right?"

"As well as you could expect, I guess."

"I suppose they kept you with the women."

"Well, we were on the move most of the time."

"I mean when you camped."

"No, not all the time."

"Did they—bother you?"

"Well," the McLaren girl said, "I guess the whole thing was kind of a bother, but I hadn't thought of it that way. One of the women cut my hair off. I don't know why. It's just now starting to grow back."

"I meant did they *bother* you?" Mrs. Favor said.

Braden was looking right at her. "You can talk plainer than that," he said.

Mrs. Favor pretended she didn't hear him. She kept her eyes on the McLaren girl and you could see what she was trying to get at. Finally she said, "You hear so many stories about what Indians do to white women."

"They do the same thing to them they do to Indian women," Braden said, and after that no one spoke for a minute. All the sounds, the rattling and the wind hissing by, were outside. Inside it was quiet.

I kept thinking that somebody ought to say something to change the subject. In the first place I felt uneasy with the talk about Apaches and John Russell sitting there. Second, I thought Braden certainly shouldn't have said what he did with ladies present, even if Mrs. Favor had started it. I thought Dr. Favor would say something to her again, but he didn't. He could have been seven hundred miles away, his hand holding the side curtain open a little and staring out at the darkness.

I would like to have said that I thought Mr. Braden should be reminded that there were ladies present, but instead I said, "I don't know if the ladies enjoy this kind of talk very much." That was a mistake.

Braden said, "What kind of talk?"

"I mean about Apache Indians and all."

"That's not what you meant," Braden said.

"Mr. Braden." The McLaren girl, her hands folded in her lap, was looking directly at him. "Why don't you just be quiet for a while?"

Braden was surprised, as all of us were, I suppose. He said, "You speak right up, don't you?"

"I don't see any other way," she said.

"I was talking to that boy next to you."

"But it concerned me," the McLaren girl said. "So if you'd be so kind as to shut up, I'd appreciate it."

That was something for her to say. The only trouble was, it egged Braden on. "A nice girl talking like that," he said, watching her. "Maybe you lived with them too long. Maybe that's it. You live with them a while and you forget how a white person talks."

I couldn't see Russell's face or his reaction to all this. But a minute later I could see what was going to happen, and I began thinking every which way of how to change the subject.

"A white woman," Mrs. Favor said, "couldn't live the way they do. The Apache woman rubbing skins and grinding corn, their hair greasy and full of vermin. The men no better. All of them standing around or squatting, picking at themselves and the dogs sniffing them. They even eat the dogs sometimes."

She was watching the McLaren girl again, leading up to something, but I wasn't sure what. "I wonder," she said, "if a woman could fall into their ways and after a while it wouldn't bother her.

Like eating with your fingers. Or do you suppose you could eat a dog and not think anything of it?"

Here's where you could see it coming.

John Russell said, "What if you didn't have anything else to eat?" This was the first time he'd spoken since we left Sweetmary. His voice was calm, but still there was an edge to it.

Mrs. Favor looked from the McLaren girl to Russell.

"I don't care how hungry I got. I know I wouldn't eat one of those camp dogs."

"I think," John Russell said, "you have to know the hunger they feel before you can be sure."

"The government supplies them with meat," Mrs. Favor said. "Every week or so I'd see them come in for their beef ration. And they're allowed to hunt. They can hunt whenever their rations are low."

"But they are always low," Russell said. "Or used up, and there's not game enough to take care of everybody."

"You hear all kinds of stories of how the Indian is oppressed by the white man," Dr. Favor said. I was surprised that he had been listening and seemed interested now.

He said, "I suppose you will always hear those stories as long as there is sympathy for the Indian's plight, and that's a good thing. But you have to live on a reservation for a time, like San Carlos, to see that caring for Indians is not a simple matter of giving them food and clothing."

He was watching John Russell all the while and seemed to be picking his words carefully. "You see all the problems then that the Interior Department is faced with," he said. "The natural resentment on the part of the Indians, their distrust, their reluctance to cultivate the soil."

"Having to live where they don't want to live," John Russell said.

"That too," Dr. Favor agreed. "Which can't be helped for the time being." His eyes were still on Russell. "Do you happen to know someone at San Carlos?"

"Many of them," Russell said.

"You've visited the agency?"

"I lived there. For three years."

"I didn't think I recognized you," Dr. Favor said. "Did you work for one of the suppliers?"

"On the police," Russell said.

Dr. Favor didn't say anything. I couldn't see his expression in the dimness, only that he was still looking at Russell.

Then his wife said, "But the police are all Apaches."

She stopped there, and all you heard was the rattling and creaking and wind rushing past and the muffled pounding of the horses.

I thought, Now he'll explain it. Whether he thinks they'll believe him or not, at least he'll say something.

But John Russell didn't say a word. Not one single word. Maybe he's thinking how to explain it, I thought. There was no way of knowing that. But he must have been thinking something and I would have given anything to know what it was. How he could just sit there in that silence was the hardest thing I have ever tried to figure out.

Finally Mrs. Favor said, "Well, I guess you never know."

You never know what? I thought. You never know a lot of things. Still, it was pretty plain what she meant.

Braden was looking at me. He said, "You let anybody on your stage?"

"I don't work for the company anymore," I answered. I'll admit, it was a weak-sister thing to say, but why should I stick up for Russell?

This wasn't any of my business. He couldn't help the ex-soldier, saying it was none of his business. All right, this was none of my business. If he wanted to act like an uncivilized person—which is what he must be and you could see it clearer all the time—then let him alone. Let him act any way he wanted.

I wasn't his father. He was full grown. So let him talk for himself if he had anything to say.

But maybe he even thought he really was Apache. That had never occurred to me before. It would have been something to look into his mind. Not for long. Not for more than a few minutes; just time enough to look around with his eyes, around and back at things that had happened to him. That would tell you a few things.

I started to think of the stories Henry Mendez had told about Russell, piecing little bits of it together now.

How he had been Juan something living in a Mexican pueblo before the Apaches came raiding and took some of the women and children. How he had been named *Ish-kay-nay* and brought up by these Chiricahuas and made the son of Sonsichay, one of the sub-chiefs of the band. Five years with them and he must have learned an awful lot.

Then, after that, living in Contention with Mr. James Russell until he was about sixteen. He had gone to school there. And he had almost killed a boy in a fight. Maybe there was a good reason he did it. But he had left soon after, so maybe there wasn't a good reason; maybe he just couldn't be taught anything.

Then the most interesting part. How John Russell got his next name, *Tres Hombres*.

He had been with the mule packers on that campaign of the Third Cavalry's, chasing down into Mexico after the bands of Chato and Chihuahua, and he got his new name in a meadow high in the Sierra Madre, two days west of the village of Tesorababi.

He had gone out looking for these mule packers who had wandered off the trail, hunting them all day and finding them, three *mozos* and eighteen mules, an hour before dark and a moment before the sudden gunfire came out of the canyon walls and caught them and ended four of the mules.

John Russell, who was sometimes Juan or Juanito, but more often *Ish-kay-nay* to the older ones of the Apache Police, shot six more of the mules in the moments that followed and he and the *mozos* laid behind the dead mules all night and all the next day. The Apaches, nine or ten of them, came twice. Running and screaming the first time they left two dead before they could creep back out of range of John Russell's Spencer. That was the evening of the first day. They came again at dawn, silently through the rocks with their bodies mud-streaked and branches of mesquite in their head-bands. They said that John Russell, with the Spencer steadied on the neck of a dead mule, waited until he was sure. He fired seven times with the Spencer, taking his time as they came at him, and emptied his Colt revolver at them as they ran. Maybe two more were hit.

The packers, their eyes closed and their bodies tight against the mules while the firing was going on, smiled at John Russell and laughed with relief at their fear when it was over. And, when they returned to the main column, they told how this one had fought like three men against ten times as many of the barbarians. From then on, among the Apache Police at San Carlos, the trackers at Fort Apache and Cibucu, John Russell was known as *Tres Hombres*.

But knowing all this wasn't the same as seeing things through his eyes. Maybe his past relations with white people explained why he acted the way he did, why he didn't speak up now, but I'm not sure. Maybe you can see it.

It was colder later on, so I got the two robes from the floor and handed one of them to Dr. Favor. He took it and his wife spread it out so it would cover Frank Braden too. I unfolded the other robe for our seat. There was the soft clicking sound of the McLaren girl's beads as she raised her hands. She gathered the end of the robe close to her, wedging it against her leg and not offering any of it to John Russell. I even had the feeling she had moved closer to me, but I wasn't sure.

I heard Dr. Favor say something to his wife; the sound not the words. She told him not to be silly. I asked the McLaren girl if she was comfortable. She said, yes, thank you. Mostly though, no one spoke. It was a lot colder and the canvas curtains, that

were all the way down now, would be flat one
minute, then snap and billow out with the wind
and through the opening you could see the darkness and shapes now and then going by alongside
the road.

Frank Braden had eased lower in the seat and
his head was very close to Mrs. Favor's. He said
something to her, a low murmur. She laughed, not
out loud, almost to herself, but you could hear it.
Her head moved to his and she said one word or
maybe a couple. Their faces were close together for
a long time, maybe even touching, and yet her husband was right there. Figure that one out.

We came in to Delgado's Station with the slowing,
braking sound of the coach coming off the slope
that stretched out toward a wall of trees and the
adobes that showed faintly against the trees. The
coach kept rolling slower and slower and slower,
with the sound of the horses getting clear and
heavy, and finally we stopped. We sat there in silence and when Mrs. Favor said, "Where are we?"
in just a whisper, it sounded loud inside that coach
in the darkness. No one answered until we heard
Henry Mendez outside.

"Delgado!" he yelled.

Then close on it came the sound of his steps and
the door opened. "Delgado's Station," Mendez

said. He stood there holding his leather bag. Beyond him, a man was coming out of the adobe carrying a lantern.

"Mendez?" The man raised the lantern.

"Who else?" Mendez said. "You still got horses?"

"For a few more days," Delgado, the stationmaster, answered.

"Change them for these."

"You got a stage?"

"A long story," Mendez said. "Get your woman to make coffee."

Delgado was frowning. He wore pants with striped suspenders over his underwear. "How do I know you're coming?"

"Just move your people," Mendez said. He turned to the coach again. "You wash at the bench by the door. You follow the path around back for other things." He offered his hand and Mrs. Favor got out. Then the McLaren girl.

"Twice in one night," Delgado said. "An hour ago we are in bed and three men come by."

"You should have stayed up," Mendez said.

Mr. Favor was just getting out of the coach. "Did you know them?" he asked.

"Some riders."

"But did you know them?"

Delgado looked thoughtful. "I don't know. I think they work for Mr. Wolgast."

"Is that usual," Dr. Favor said, "them coming by this time of night?"

"Man, it happens," Delgado said. "People go by here."

By the time I went around back and came out again, just Mendez and Russell were standing there. Mendez took a bottle that looked like brandy out of his leather bag and both of them had a long drink.

Two boys, in shirts and pants but barefooted, came out of the adobe. Both of them smiled at Mendez and one of them called, "Hey, Tio, what have you got?"

"Something for your grease pails," Mendez said, "and the need of clean horses." The boys ran off again, around the adobe, and Mendez turned to John Russell again.

"How do you like a mud wagon?"

Russell said something in Spanish.

"How do you like it in English?" Mendez said.

"That again," Russell said.

"Practice, uh? Then you get good."

"Maybe if I don't speak it's better."

"And what does that mean?" Mendez asked.

Russell didn't say anything. One of the boys came running out again with a bucket and Mendez said, "Paint them good, *chico*."

"This costs more at night," the boy said, still smiling, as if still smiling from before.

"I'll pay you with something," Mendez said. He took a swipe at the boy with the leather bag, but the boy got past him. Then he offered the brandy to Russell again. "For the dust," he said. "Or whatever reason you want."

While Russell was taking a drink, Mendez saw me and offered me one, so I joined them and had a swallow. It was all right, except it was so hot. I don't know how they took the big swigs they did. Mendez took his turn then handed the bottle to Russell and went into the adobe.

The Mexican boy with the grease pail was working on the front wheels now. The other boy had unhitched the lead team and was taking the horses off. We watched them a while. Then I said, "How come you didn't tell them?"

He looked at me, holding the bottle. "Tell them what?"

"That you're not what they think."

His eyes looked at me another second. Then he took a drink of the brandy.

"You want to go in?" I said. He just shrugged.

We went in then—into a low-ceilinged room that was lighted by one lantern hanging from a beam; the lantern had smoked and there was still the oil smell of it in the room.

The Favors and the McLaren girl and Braden were sitting at the main table, a long plank one in the middle of the room. Mendez stood there like he

had been talking to them. But he moved away as
we came in and motioned us over to a table by the
kitchen door. Delgado's wife came out with a pot
of coffee, but went over to the main table before
pouring us some. Mendez waited, looking at Russell all the while, until she went out to the kitchen
again.

"They think you're Apache," he said.

Russell didn't say anything. He was looking at
the brandy bottle as if reading the small print.
Mendez picked up the brandy and poured some of
it in his coffee.

"You hear what I said?"

"Does it make a difference?" Russell said then.

"Dr. Favor says you shouldn't ride in the
coach," Mendez said. "That's the difference."

Russell's eyes raised to Mendez. "They all say
that?"

"Listen, you wanted to ride with me before."

"Do they all say I shouldn't be in the coach?"

Mendez nodded. "Dr. Favor said they agreed to
it. I said this boy isn't Apache, did you ask if he
was? Did you ask him anything? But this Favor
says he isn't going to argue about it."

Russell kept looking at Mendez. "What did you
say?"

"Well—I don't know," Mendez said. "Why have
people unhappy? Why not just"—he shrugged—
"let them have their way? It isn't a big thing. I

mean I don't know if it's something worth making trouble about. He's got this in his mind now and we don't have time to convince him of the truth. So why should we let it worry us, uh?"

"What if I want to ride in the coach?" Russell said.

"Listen, you wanted to ride with me before. Why all of a sudden you like it inside now?"

It was the first time I ever saw Mendez look worried, like something was happening that he couldn't handle or have an answer for. He drank some of his coffee, but looked up quickly, holding the cup, as Braden and Dr. Favor rose from the table. Braden went outside. Dr. Favor went over to the bar where Delgado was, and Mendez seemed to relax a little and sip his coffee.

"Is it worth arguing about?" Mendez said. "Getting people upset and angry? Sure, they're wrong. But is it easier to convince them of it or just forget about it? You understand that?"

"I'm learning," Russell said.

Right there, again, I'd like to have seen what was going on in his mind, because you certainly couldn't tell from his tone. He had such a quiet way of speaking you got the feeling nothing in the world would ever bother him.

While we were still sitting there, Dr. Favor motioned Mendez over to the bar where he and Delgado were. Mendez stood there talking to them for a long time, while we finished our coffee and had another. Finally Mendez came back. He didn't sit down but took a drink of the brandy.

"Dr. Favor wants to go another way," Mendez said. "The road down past the old San Pete Mine."

It was a road Hatch & Hodges had used years before when the mine was still in operation. It ran fifteen or so miles east of the main road, through foothills and on up into high country past the mine, then it joined the present main road again on the way to Benson. But I had never heard of anyone taking it these days. The country through there was wild and climbing, harder to travel over. That's why the new road had been put through after the mine shut down. The only thing you could say about the old road was it was shorter.

But was that reason to take it?

Mendez said why not? Delgado was sure the rest of the stations along the main road had already shut down. At least all their change horses had been moved south by now. Delgado was the only one left with any and his would be gone in a few days. If we have only six horses and there are no more stations, Mendez said. Why not go the short way?

That made sense. We'd have to bring extra food and water, though. Mendez agreed to that. He said as long as Dr. Favor was paying for most of this, why not keep him happy? (Henry Mendez seemed very anxious to keep people happy.)

"Maybe he's a little worried too," Mendez said. "He was talking to Delgado again about those people who came by here. What did they look like? Did they say where they were going? Things like that."

"If he thinks they plan to hold us up," I said, "they couldn't. They wouldn't know a stage was coming by here tonight."

"I told him that," Mendez said. "He said, 'If there is a possibility of being stopped, we should take precautions.' I said, 'Maybe, but, if this was the regular stage, we wouldn't even be talking about it.'"

"Maybe he is really worried," I said.

Mendez nodded. "Like something's after him. And he knows it."

A little later, after Mendez had seen about the provisions and water bags, we got moving again. Frank Braden was already in the coach asleep with his feet on the seat across from him. We just let him be. There was room enough with John Russell up on the boot now.

Soon we were alone in the night with the rumbling and creaking sounds. We turned off the road about two miles south of Delgado's and went through a mesquite thicket with the branches scraping both sides of the coach. Then this trail opened up and you could feel it beginning to climb. We would move through trees, in and out of close darkness, all the time following the winding, climbing road that led on and on, two rutted tracks that were overgrown but I guess still visible to Mendez.

About three hours out of Delgado's, Mendez and Russell changed the teams, giving the two spares a turn in the harness, and watering them. I was the only one who got out of the coach, though I'm sure Dr. Favor was awake too. I had a drink of water from Mendez's canteen (this was kept in the driver's boot; three hide bags of water on the back end were for the passengers and the horses) and then we were off again.

I went to sleep after that, wondering for the longest time if the McLaren girl would say anything if I was to put my arm around her. I never did find out.

With the first signs of daylight and down out of a winding, steep-sided canyon, we came to the abandoned San Pete mine. Mendez and Russell were standing there as we got out, everybody stretching, feeling the stiffness from being cramped up so long, and looking around at the company buildings.

The ones near us were built against the slope so that the front verandas were on stilts and high as a second floor. Out across the canyon the mine works were about two hundred yards off: the crushing mill part way up the slope, the ore tailings that humped in hogbacks down from the mine shaft way up higher. Braden was looking at Mendez. "This isn't the stage road," he said.

"We took a different way," Mendez answered. He was at the back untying one of the waterskins.

"What do you mean a different way?"

I noticed John Russell step away from the horses. He watched Braden move toward Mendez who was lifting the waterskin to his shoulder.

"You take any road you feel like?"

"Talk to Dr. Favor," Mendez said.

"I'm talking to you."

Mendez had started for the building, but he stopped. "The others agreed on it," he said. "You were asleep. But I thought, if he wants to come with us so bad then this is all right with him."

Braden kept watching him. "Where does it lead?"

"Same places," Mendez answered. He took the waterskin under the veranda and came out again stretching, looking up at the sky that was still dull though streaked with traces of sunlight above the far end of the canyon. "We eat now," Mendez said. "Then rest for two hours."

Dr. Favor said, "If you're thinking of us—"

"More of the horses," Mendez said. "And me."

We ate breakfast under the veranda of the main

company building, some of the bread and cold meat and coffee Mendez had brought. And after Mendez took his blanket roll to the next house, the only one besides the main one that still had a roof. John Russell went with him and they slept for a couple of hours.

So there was nothing to do but wait during that time. The mud wagon stood alone with the horses grazing farther down the canyon where there was grass and some owl clover. After a while Frank Braden walked out past the coach, gazing at the slope above the mine works, then looking up-canyon, the way he had come. He went on getting smaller and smaller as he crossed the canyon and got up by the crushing mill. He kept going, finally reaching what looked like an assay shack high up by the mine shaft and you couldn't see him any more. I wondered if he was waiting for Mrs. Favor to come up. That or he was just restless.

Whichever, Braden was back in plenty of time. He had calmed down and he asked Mendez how long it would take to reach Benson. Mendez told him this way was shorter than the stage road, but we had the horses to consider. So maybe it would take just as long, arriving in Benson sometime to-morrow morning if the road was all right and if nothing happened.

Well, we left the San Pete mine before eight o'clock and by midnight the first *if* came true.

The trouble was not in following the road, a matter of whether or not the road was "all right." There was just no road to follow. We crossed a shallow arroyo that came down out of the high rocks, and on the other side, where the road should have continued, there was no trace of it.

Wind and rock slides and flash floods had worn the road away or covered it or wiped it clean from the slope. Mendez had no choice. He took the coach down the arroyo, bucking, fighting down through the yellow *palo verdes* that grew along the banks waiting for water, then south again, out into the flat brush country to circle the dry washes and rock formations that extended out from the slopes.

The land lay dead in the heat of the sun, bone dry and thick with greasewood and prickly pear and tall saguaro that looked like fence posts growing wild. Henry Mendez did a good job driving through this, but it took forever. You would look ahead and see an outcropping of rock or a scattering of Joshua trees that looked only a few hundred yards off, but it would take even an hour to reach them and after passing them there would be other marks on the land, like a strangely shaped giant saguaro or more Joshuas or yucca, that would take forever to reach and finally pass. There was nothing to look at, nothing to look forward to.

We stopped to alternate the horses once during the morning, discovering only two waterskins on the back end. We had left one, more than half full, at the San Pete mine.

We stopped again at noon, all of us standing by the coach waiting for the coffee water to boil, Mendez unhitching the teams and feeding them from morrals, Mendez probably waiting for one of the passengers to say this was crazy and why didn't we go back to the stage road? Lose a day, but at least not have to put up with this. But no one said it.

It was strange. There was Mrs. Favor saying it was hot, saying it different ways, but not seeming to mind it. She would glance now and then at the McLaren girl, probably still wondering what the Indians did to her, then look at Braden who had turned quiet today and seemed a different person, as if the effects of whisky had worn off him (though I am not saying he showed any signs of drunkenness the day before). There was the McLaren girl, seeming to be the most patient, aside from Russell (how could it bother him to be out here), and Dr. Favor who watched Mendez, trying to hurry him with his eyes. Nobody asked Mendez if we might get lost or break down. Nobody seemed worried at all. Not even about having left some of our water behind at the San Pete.

We went on, and it was afternoon before we got out of that flat country. Mendez saw the road again up on the slope, a trace of it cutting through the brush, and headed for it. You could see the hills getting bigger and clearer as we approached, shadowed and dark with brush and washes, but up above the peaks looked bare and silent in the sunlight.

We got up to the road and followed it easily for a while, but then it started to climb again, getting higher up into the hills, and finally Mendez pulled in the team.

He leaned down and said, "Everybody takes a nice walk. To the top of the grade."

We got out, all of us looking up, seeing a pretty steep section ahead. Russell was already walking up it, I guess making sure there weren't any washouts we couldn't see from here. The slope wasn't too steep, but Mendez, you could tell, was thinking of the horses.

So we waited until the coach and trailing horses were past us a ways and then started up. Dr. Favor took his wife's arm as if to help her walking, but I think it was so she wouldn't wander off. Frank Braden stood there to make a cigarette, so I fell in with the McLaren girl, thinking hard of something to say. But I didn't have to think for more than a few steps.

She said, "He doesn't look Apache, does he?" as if she'd started right in the middle of her thoughts.

But even that abruptly I knew she was talking about Russell. No question about it. She was squinting a little in the sunlight, looking at him way up on the road.

"You should have seen him a few weeks ago," I said.

She looked at me, waiting for me to explain, and I was a little sorry I'd said it. Still, it was a fact.

"He looked like any other Indian on Army pay."

"Then he *is* Apache?"

"Well, maybe you can't answer that yes or no."

She was frowning a little. "Mr. Mendez said he isn't. That's what I don't understand."

"Well, he wasn't born one. But he's lived with them so long, I mean by his own choice, that maybe he is one by now."

"But why," she said, "would anybody *want* to be one?"

"That's it," I said. "Wanting to be one is just as bad as being one. Maybe worse."

"But wanting to live the way they do," she said.

"You'd have to see things with his eyes to understand that."

"I think I'd be afraid to," she said.

I wanted to say that I didn't think she'd be afraid of anything after what she'd been through, but then thought it best to stay wide of that subject. It could be embarrassing for her. She had talked a little about it in the coach and hadn't seemed embarrassed, but still there could be touchy things. It was like being with a person who

has a great big nose or something. You don't want
to get caught looking at the nose or even saying the
word. (I hope no one reading this who might have
a big nose will take offense. I wasn't making fun of
noses.)

The trailing horses were still on the grade, but
the coach had passed over the crest and stopped.
You could only see the top part of it at first. The
road leveled into pinyon and a lot of brush, and on
the right side, slanting down at the coach, was a
steep cutbank about seven or eight feet high.

"I guess we can get in again," the girl said.

I heard her, but I was watching Mendez. He was
looking up at the top of the bank.

We walked around the trailing horses and I
looked up there too. My first thought was, what is
Russell doing sitting up there? And where did he
get the rifle?

Then I saw Russell, not on the cutbank but beyond the Favors and up by the teams. Near him, at
the banked side of the road was another man,
holding a revolver. I guess the McLaren girl saw
them the same time I did, but she didn't let out a
peep.

What is there to say, for that matter? You walk
up a road out in the middle of nowhere and there
are two armed men waiting for you. Even though
you know something is wrong, you act as if this
happens every day and twice on Sunday. I mean

you don't get excited or act surprised. You just hold yourself in and maybe they will go away if you don't admit they are there. You don't think at the time: I am afraid. You are too busy acting natural.

The man on the bank came down to the edge and squatted there holding the rifle (it was a Henry) on us until we were up even with the coach. Then he jumped down to the road, almost falling, and as he stood up I recognized him at once.

It was the one named Lamarr Dean who rode for Mr. Wolgast. And the other one up by Russell, sure enough, was Early. The same two who had been at Delgado's the first time I ever saw John Russell.

What if they recognize him, I thought. Not—what's going on? Or what are they doing here? But—what if they recognize him? I couldn't help thinking that first because I remembered so well how Russell had broken that whisky glass against Lamarr Dean's mouth. Lamarr Dean must have remembered it even better. But he hadn't recognized him. Early hadn't either, else he wouldn't have just been standing there holding that long-barreled revolver.

Mendez, looking down at Lamarr Dean, said, "You better think before you do something."

"Step down off there and don't worry about it,"

Lamarr Dean said. Mendez climbed down and Lamarr Dean looked over toward us. He waited; I didn't know why until Braden came up past us and Lamarr Dean's eyes followed him. He said, "We like to not made it."

"I kept thinking," Braden said, "they got some catching up to do once they find the way."

"When you didn't come by the main road." Lamarr Dean said, "we went back to Delgado's early this morning. I said to him, 'Are we hearing things or was that a coach passed us last night?' He said, 'You must have been hearing things; there was a coach but it wasn't on the main road.' 'Which way did it go?' I said and that was when he told me you'd taken this other way and I'll tell you we done some riding."

I kept looking at Braden all the time Lamarr Dean was talking. Maybe you aren't surprised now why Braden took the stage in the first place and was so anxious to be on it when we left Sweetmary. It is easy to think back and say I knew it all the time. But I'll tell you I couldn't believe it at first. Braden was not a person you liked, but he was one of us, a passenger like everybody else, and, when he showed himself to be part of this holdup, it must have surprised the others as much as it did me. Though at the time I didn't look to see their reaction. Too much was going on.

Early came over, not saying anything, his face

dark with beard growth. He was prodding Russell ahead of him.

Then another man appeared. He looked like a Mexican and wore a straw hat. He was mounted and walked his horse out of the trees, leading two other saddled horses, and stood there in front of the teams. I noticed he wore two .44 revolvers.

Lamarr Dean stood with his hand through the lever of the Henry, his finger on the trigger, but the barrel pointed down and almost touching the ground.

"Old Dr. Favor's pretending he don't see us," Lamarr Dean said.

He moved me aside and motioned the McLaren girl over against the cutbank. "You all spread out so I can see my old friend." Dean was looking directly at Dr. Favor then. "Things start to close in on you?" he asked.

"I'm afraid you're beyond me," Dr. Favor said, though not sounding surprised.

"Ahead of you," Lamarr Dean said. "I've seen this coming for two, three months."

"You've seen what coming?"

"Frank, he's still pretending."

Braden came up beside Lamarr Dean. "He's used to it."

"We're going to Bisbee," Dr. Favor said. "On business. We'll be there two days at most."

"No," Lamarr Dean said. "You'll be there just

long enough to get a ride south. You'll hole up in Mexico or else get a boat in Vera Cruz and head out."

"You're sure of that," Dr. Favor said.

"That's how it's done."

"And if I deny it, tell you we're going back in two days?"

"What's the sense?"

"He should be over here with a gun," Braden said.

"No," Lamarr Dean said. "He uses his ink pen. All you do is write down a higher beef tally than what comes in. Pay the trail driver U.S. government scrip for what's delivered and keep the over-payment. Isn't that right, Doctor?"

"Like he never saw you before," Braden said.

Lamarr Dean looked at Mrs. Favor. "You pretending too?"

"I know you," she said, pretty calmly, considering everything. "But I don't remember him," nodding to Braden.

"No, Frank wasn't anywhere near. He was still in Yuma then."

"I guess that's enough," Braden said. "We got things to do."

"I was just trying to understand it," Mrs. Favor said easily. Her eyes shifted to Lamarr Dean who she knew by now was the talker among them.

"You were working for the man who had the contract to supply beef."

"Mr. Wolgast."

"And you found out about my husband."

"Audra," Dr. Favor said, sounding unconcerned
but hardly taking his eyes from Lamarr Dean or
Braden, while the rest of us couldn't help but
watch him. (My gosh, the things we were learning
all of a sudden!) "Audra," he said, "you know we
don't have to talk about our personal business to
these people."

Braden moved away. "Let's get to it," he said
and nodded to Early who started unhitching the
team horses. As he stripped off the harness and
brought them out, slapping them and keeping
them moving, the Mexican, who was still
mounted, bunched the horses and started them
along.

The road formed two tracks out across a grassy
meadow that was wide, pretty wide across and
stetched on at least a mile with slopes rising up on
both sides. As soon as the Mexican was off a ways,
Early mounted up again and started after him.

Braden was behind the coach now and we saw
just part of him as he yanked down the canvas and
started pulling the bags off.

Lamarr Dean started looking us over then, I
mean to see if we were armed. He took a revolver

from inside Dr. Favor's coat, a small caliber gun that he studied for a minute then threw off into the brush on the other side of the road. He went on to Mendez, passing Mrs. Favor and the McLaren girl, and Mendez opened his coat to show he was unarmed.

"What about up in the boot?" Lamarr Dean asked.

"A shotgun," Mendez said.

"See it stays there and you here," Lamarr Dean said. He came on to me and I opened my coat as Mendez had done.

As Lamarr Dean looked me over Mendez said, "You think it's worth it? You won't be able to show your face again."

"I appreciate it," Lamarr said, "but don't give me no advice please."

"I would bet you're dead or arrested in two weeks," Mendez said.

Lamarr glanced at him now. "You won't have nothing to bet with."

"All right, then remember it," Mendez said. "You already have witnesses."

"I don't see any," Lamarr Dean said. Braden came from behind the coach with a leather satchel. "Frank, you see any witnesses?"

"Not here," Braden said. He knelt down to open the satchel.

Lamarr Dean moved on to Russell. "This one

doesn't look like any witness to me. Mister,"
Lamarr said, "are you a witness?" He pulled Russell's Colt as he said it and flung it backhanded,
high up so that it glinted with the sun catching it,
and down the road, bouncing and skidding way
down it.

But Lamarr Dean wasn't watching the gun. He
was staring at Russell, up close to him and squinting, looking right in his face.

"I've seen you somewhere," Lamarr said. The
way he said it you knew it bothered him. He
waited for Russell to help him, but Russell didn't
say a word. They stared at each other and every
second you expected Lamarr to remember that day
at Delgado's, and you could just imagine him suddenly swinging that Henry rifle up and giving Russell the same thing Russell gave him, or worse.

Or Braden might say something about "the Indian" and then Lamarr Dean would remember.
You waited for that to happen too. But, when
Braden looked up, the bag open on the ground in
front of him, he said, "I'd say it was a good day's
pay."

Lamarr Dean looked from Braden over to Dr.
Favor. "How much you steal so we won't have to
count it?"

Dr. Favor didn't say anything. He was a man in
a dark suit and hat standing there watching, with
one thumb hooked in a vest pocket and the other

hand at his side. The McLaren girl, Mrs. Favor, Mendez, John Russell—all of them in fact just stood there patiently, as if they had stopped by to watch but didn't have anything to do with what was going on.

"He figures he's helped out enough without giving us a tally," Braden said. He rose, handing the satchel to Dean who took it and transferred the currency to his saddlebags.

"About twelve thousand I figured," Lamarr Dean said.

"Somewhere around it," Braden said.

"He did all right," Lamarr Dean said. "But I guess we did better." He saw Braden looking at the two horses that still trailed the coach on a line. "What do you think?" he said then.

"I guess they'll do." Braden looked up at the coach. "And the two saddles."

Lamarr Dean looked at him. "What do you need two for?"

"You'll see," Braden said. He motioned to me. "You get them down."

That's how I came to be up on the coach when they rode out. I threw down Braden's saddle, then Russell's, looking at him as I did.

Russell watched, not saying a word as Braden freed the line and pulled in the horses and slipped the hackamores off them. He put his own saddle on one horse and told Russell to put his on the other.

Right then I thought, they're taking Russell along as a hostage. It made sense; they hadn't bothered us up to now, but they certainly weren't going to be so kind as to just ride off. Which turned out to be right. Only it wasn't Russell they took.

It was Mrs. Favor. Braden brought the horse over to her and said, "I thought you'd come along with us a ways," sounding nice about it.

And just as nice she said, "I'd better not," as if they were discussing it and she had a choice.

Braden held out his hand. "You'll be all right."

"I'll be all right here," Mrs. Favor said.

Braden stared at her. "You're coming, one way or the other." And that was the end of the discussion.

He helped her up, Mrs. Favor holding the skirt to cover her legs as she sat the saddle, and they moved off down the road. Braden stayed close to her and neither of them looked back. We all kept watching, nobody saying anything. Dr. Favor in fact didn't say anything even before, when Braden was forcing his wife to go with him.

Lamarr Dean mounted up then. He sat there cradling the Henry across his arms, looking down at the people there and finally up to me, thinking about something, maybe wanting to be sure he hadn't made any mistakes.

He thought of one thing. "The shotgun," he said. "Open it up and throw it away."

I climbed down to the driver's seat and did as I was told, emptying both shells before heaving the gun off into the brush. Lamarr Dean nodded. He wheeled around and took off after Braden and Mrs. Favor, not hurrying though.

By now Braden and Mrs. Favor were about a hundred yards off, out in the wide-open part of the meadow. Way off beyond them there was just dust to show that Early and the Mexican were up there somewhere driving the horse teams.

I felt the coach shake; I remember that. But I didn't look around till a moment later. When I did, there was John Russell kneeling on the roof right behind me unbuckling the cartridge belt from his blanket roll. He glanced up, keeping an eye on Dean who was taking his time moving away from us. Russell slipped the Spencer out, looking at Lamarr Dean again, and that was when he spoke.

He said, "How do they get that sure of themselves?"

I didn't know what he meant, and certainly couldn't believe he intended to shoot Lamarr Dean. I said, "What?"

"How do they get that sure with the mistakes they make?" Already he was slipping a cartridge into the breech, loading it quick for single fire. I guess I didn't say anything then.

He was busy and it was like he was telling it to himself. "Luck then," he said. "They think they know how to do it, but it's luck." I saw him slip three cartridges from the belt and hold them in his left hand. All of a sudden he held still.

I looked around and saw Dean riding back toward us. Braden and Mrs. Favor, two hundred yards off, had come around and reined in as if to wait for him.

Lamarr Dean had put his rifle in the saddle boot, but now, as he approached us, he drew his Colt.

3

Lamarr Dean was close now.

"I pretty near forgot something," he said. Then he noticed Russell up on the roof behind me. "What're you at up there?"

"Getting my things," John Russell said. The Spencer was down between his legs as he knelt there, sitting back on his feet, his hands flat on his thighs.

"Expect you're going somewhere?"

"Well," Russell shrugged, "why sit here, uh?"

"How far you think you'll get?"

"That's something to find out."

Lamarr Dean heeled his horse, moving to the back of the coach. He stood up in the stirrups to reach one of the two waterskins hanging there, unhooked it, and looped the end thong over his saddle horn. Then he came back with the skin hanging round and tight in front of his left leg. He pulled the horse around so he was facing us again.

"You didn't say how far you'd get," Lamarr Dean said.

Russell's shoulders went up and down. "We find that out after a while."

Lamarr Dean raised the revolver, hesitating, making sure we saw what he was going to do. Mendez yelled something. I'm not sure what, maybe just a sound. But as he yelled it, Lamarr Dean pulled the trigger and the waterskin still hanging from the back of the coach burst open. It gushed and then trickled as the bag sagged, all the water wasting itself on that sandy road, and Lamarr Dean just sat there looking at us. He didn't smile or laugh, but you could see he enjoyed it.

He said to Russell, "Now how far?"

There wasn't supposed to be an answer to that. Lamarr Dean took up his reins and started around. Russell waited till that moment.

"Maybe," he said, "as far as Delgado's."

Lamarr Dean held up, taken off-stride, and now he was sideways to us, his gun hand on the offside and he had to turn his head around over his shoulder to look up at Russell.

"You said something?"

"Maybe if we get thirsty," Russell said, "we'll go to Delgado's and have *mescal*."

Lamarr Dean didn't move, even with his head turned in that awkward position. He stared up at Russell, and I'm certain that right then something was dawning on him.

He said, "You do that." For a few more seconds

he looked up at Russell, then nudged his horse and started off again with his back to us and holding to a walking pace to show that he wasn't afraid of anything.

I kept watching him—thirty, forty, fifty feet away then, about that far when Russell's voice said, "Get down," not suddenly, but calmly and in a quiet tone.

I dropped down on the seat, ducking my head, and Russell said, "All the way *down*—"

And that last word wasn't quiet, still it wasn't yelled or excited. I saw the Spencer suddenly up to his face and I dropped, looking around to see where I was going and catching a glimpse of Lamarr Dean sixty feet out and wheeling his mount and bringing the Colt gun straight out in front of him, thinking he had time to be sure and *bam* the Spencer went off in my ear and Lamarr Dean went out of that saddle like he'd been clubbed in the face, his horse swerving, then running.

Russell must have been sure of his shot, for he was already reloaded and tracking the horse, and, when he fired, the horse stumbled and rolled and tried to get up. And out past the horse you could see Braden coming in. Coming, then swerving as that Spencer went off again, banging hard close to me and cracking thin out in the open. There was

the sound of Braden's revolver twice and I hugged
the floor of the boot, looking up to see just the barrel of the Spencer. Russell was full length behind it
now, resting the barrel on the front rail, tracking
Braden with the sights and not hurrying his fire.
Braden swerved again and this time kept going all
the way around full circle and back the way he had
come toward the small figure way out there that
was Mrs. Favor, so you knew Russell had come
close. At least Braden didn't want any part of him
right then.

I raised up. Russell was loading again, now that
there was time, taking a loading tube from his blanket and putting seven of the .56-56 slugs in it and
shoving the tube up through the stock of the
Spencer.

"They'll all come back now," I said. "Won't
they?"

"As sure as we have what they want," Russell
said.

There was a space there where nothing happened. I
saw Dr. Favor and Mendez and the McLaren girl,
all three of them in a row, crouched against the
cutbank where they'd gone when the shooting
started. It was quiet now, but still nobody moved.

Russell was buckling on his cartridge belt, over
his left shoulder and down across his chest, work-

ing it around so that the full cartridge loops were
all in front. While he did this, his eyes never left the
two specks way out on the meadow.

We had some time, but I did not think of it then.
Braden had to get Early and the Mexican before he
came back and they could be a mile off running the
stage horses. I kept thinking of how Russell had
brought up his Spencer and put it on Lamarr Dean,
the way a man might aim at a tin can on a fence,
and killed him with one shot. Then he had
dropped the horse that was running away with the
water bag. He had killed a man, sure of it, and in
the same second he had known he must get the
horse and he did that too.

The space where nothing happened lasted
maybe a minute altogether. Then it was over for
good.

Russell moved past me, frontwards, stepping on
the wheel and then jumping. He was carrying his
Spencer of course, and in the other hand his blanket roll and the canteen he and Mendez had used.
(Little things you remember: there was no strap on
the canteen, only two metal rings a strap had once
been fastened to, and Russell hooked a finger
through one of the rings to carry it.)

I don't think he even looked at the others, but
started off down the road we had come up, only
stopping to pick up his Colt gun and shove it in his
holster. Down just past there he left the road and

started up the slope, moving pretty quickly through the greasewood and other brush.

Dr. Favor woke up first. He yelled at Russell. Then Mendez was out on the road looking up at Russell, and Dr. Favor had run off into the brush on the other side of the coach.

I started down then, taking the grainsack our provisions were in and my blanket roll. By the time I was on the road, Dr. Favor was coming out of the brush with his little revolver and Mendez's sawed-off shotgun. Mendez and the McLaren girl were still watching Russell.

"He's running," Dr. Favor said. He was not at all calm and at that moment I thought if the shotgun was loaded he would have fired it at Russell.

"We need him," Dr. Favor said then. He knew it right then. He knew it as sure as he thought John Russell was an Apache Indian and we were afoot out in the middle of nowhere.

That's when the rest of us came wide awake. The McLaren girl said, "I wouldn't have any idea where to go. I don't think I even know where we are."

"We're maybe half way," I said. "Maybe more. If we were over on the main road I could tell."

"Then how far's the main road?"

Favor shot a look at her like he was trying to think and she had interrupted him. "Just keep quiet," he said.

It stung her, you could see. "Standing out here in the open," she said, "what good does keeping quiet do?"

Dr. Favor never answered her. He looked at Mendez and said, "Come on," handing him his shotgun, and they hurried out to where Lamarr Dean's horse was, Dr. Favor skirting around Lamarr Dean's body which lay spread-armed like it had been staked out, but Mendez stopped there to take Lamarr Dean's Colt. Then they were both at the dead horse, kneeling there a minute, Favor pulling loose the saddlebags while Mendez got the waterskin. They didn't bother with the Henry rifle, or else it was under the horse and held fast.

While they were at the dead horse, the McLaren girl said, still watching them, "He's not even thinking of his wife. Do you know that?"

"Well, sure he is," I said, not meaning he was actually thinking about her, but at least concerned about her. What did the girl expect him to do? He couldn't just chase after Braden. That wouldn't get his wife back.

"He's forgotten her," the McLaren girl said. "All he's thinking about is the money he stole."

"You can't just say something like that," I said. I meant you couldn't know what somebody was thinking, especially in the jackpot we were in right then. A person *acted*, and thought about it later.

It was getting the things from Lamarr's horse

that took time, the reason we were not right behind Russell or had him in sight anymore by the time we got down the road past the cutbank and started up the slope.

Dr. Favor, with the saddlebags over one shoulder, kept ahead of us, following the same direction Russell had taken. The slope was not very difficult at first, a big open sweep that humped up to a bunch of pines along the top; but, as we were hurrying, it wasn't long before our legs started aching and getting so tight you thought something would knot inside and you'd never get it loosened.

We were hurrying because of what was behind us, you can bet all your wages on that. But we were also hurrying to catch Russell, feeling like little kids running home in the dark and scared the house was going to be locked and nobody home. Do you see how we felt? We were worried he had left us to go on his own. In other words, knowing we needed Russell if we were going to find our way out of here alive.

When Dr. Favor reached the trees he hesitated, or seemed to, then he was gone. That's when we hurried faster, all worn out by then. You could hear Mendez breathing ten feet away.

But there was no need to hurry. As we reached the top there was Dr. Favor standing just inside the shade of the trees. Russell was just past him. He was sitting down with his blanket open on the ground and his boots off. He was pulling on a pair of curl-toed Apache moccasins, not paying any attention to Dr. Favor who stood there like he had caught Russell and was holding him from getting away, actually pointing his revolver at him. Dr. Favor's chest was moving up and down with his breathing.

Mendez moved in a little closer, watching Russell. "Why didn't you wait for us?" he said. Russell didn't bother to answer. You weren't even sure he heard Mendez.

"He doesn't care what we do," Dr. Favor said. "Long as he gets away."

"Man," Mendez said. "What's the matter with you? We have to think about this and talk it over. What if one of us just ran off? You think that would be a good thing?"

Russell raised his leg to pull a moccasin on. They were the high Apache kind, like leggings which come up past your knees. He began rolling it down, stuffing the pants leg into it and fastening it about calf-high with a strap of something. He didn't look up until he had finished this.

Then he said, "What do you want?"

"What do we want?" Mendez said, surprised. "We want to get out of here."

"What's stopping you?" Russell said.

Mendez kept frowning. "What's the matter with you?"

Russell had both moccasins on now. He took his boots and rolled them inside the blanket. Doing this, not looking at us, he said, "You want to go with me, uh?"

"With you? We all go together. This isn't happening to just one person," Mendez said. "This is happening to all of us."

"But you want me to show you the way," Russell said.

"Sure you show the way. We follow. But we're all together."

"I don't know," Russell said, very slowly, like he was thinking it over. He looked up at Dr. Favor, directly at him. "I can't ride with you. Maybe you can't walk with me . . . uh?"

For a minute, maybe even longer, nobody said a word. Russell finished rolling his blanket and tied it up with a piece of line he'd had inside.

When he stood up, Mendez said—not surprised or excited or frowning now, but so serious his voice wasn't even very loud—he said, "What does that mean?"

Russell looked at him. "It means I can't ride with them and maybe they can't walk with me. Maybe they don't walk the way I walk. You *sabe* that, Mexican?"

"I helped you like you're my own son!" Mendez's voice rose and his eyes opened so that you could see all the whites. But Russell wasn't looking. He was walking off. Mendez kept shouting, "What's the matter with you!"

"Let him go," Dr. Favor said.

We stood there watching Russell move off through the trees.

"What do you expect?" Dr. Favor said. "Do you expect somebody like that to act the way a decent person would?"

"I helped him," Mendez said, as if he couldn't believe what had happened.

"All right, now he'll help us," Dr. Favor said. "He won't have anything to do with us, but we can follow him, can't we?"

Nobody thought to try to answer that question at the time, because it wasn't really a question. I thought about it later, though. I thought about it for the next two or three hours as we tried to keep up with Russell.

It was about 3:30 or 4 o'clock when the holdup took place, with already a lot of shade on this side of the hills. From then on the light kept getting dimmer. I mean right from the time we started following Russell it was hard to keep him in sight, even when he was out in the open.

In daylight the land was spotted with brush and rock, dead and dusty looking, but with some color, light green and dark green and brown and whitish yellow. In the evening it all turned brown and hazy looking, with high peaks all around us once we'd gone on down through the other side of the pines out into open country again.

I say open, but by that I mean only there weren't any trees. I don't mean to say it was easy to travel over.

We moved along with Dr. Favor usually ahead of us. Way up ahead you would see Russell. Then you wouldn't see him. Not because he had hidden, but because of the time of day and just the way that country was, with little dips and rises and wild with all kinds of scrub brush and cactus. The saguaros that were all over didn't look like fence posts now. They were like grave markers in an Indian burial ground, if there is such a place as that. This wasn't what scared you though, it was what was coming behind us and trying to keep up with Russell that did.

He must have known we were following. But he never once ran or tried to hide on us. The McLaren girl wondered out loud why he didn't. I guess he knew he didn't have to.

There was a pass that led through these hills which Russell followed a little ways, then crossed the half mile or so of openness to the other side and headed up through a barranca that rose as a big trough between two ridges. Following him across the openness we kept looking back, but Braden and his men were not close to us yet.

Russell left the barranca, climbing again up to

the cover of trees. I think that climb was the hardest part and wore us out the most, all of us hurrying, wasting our strength as we tried to keep him in
sight. Once up on this ridge, though, there was no
sign of him.

We kept to the trees, moving north because we
figured he would. Then after a mile or so there was
the end of the trees. This hump of a ridge trailed
off into a bare spine and then we were working our
way down again into another pass, a darker, more
shadowed one, because now it was later. It was
here that we sighted Russell again, and here that
we almost gave up and said what was the use. He
was climbing again, almost up the other side of
this pass, way up past the brush to where the slope
was steep and rocky, and we knew then that we
would never keep up with him.

Dr. Favor claimed he was deliberately trying to
lose us. But the McLaren girl said no, he didn't
care if we followed or sprouted wings and flew; he
was thinking of Braden and his men on horseback
and he was making it as hard for them as he could,
making them get off their horses and walk if they
wanted to follow him.

When she said this and we thought of Braden
again, we went on, tired or not, and climbed right
up that grade Russell had, skinning ourselves
pretty bad because now it was hard to see your
footing in the dim light.

It was up on that slope, in trees again, that we rested and ate some of the dried beef and biscuits from the grainsack. Before we were through it was dark, almost as dark as it would get. This rest, which was our longest one, made it hard to get up and we started arguing about going on.

Mendez was for staying. He said going on wasn't worth it. Let Braden catch up for all he cared.

Dr. Favor said we *had* to go on, practically ordering us to. Braden would have to stop because he couldn't follow our trail in the dark. So we should take advantage of this and keep going.

Keep going, the McLaren girl said. That sounded fine. But which way? How did we know we wouldn't get turned around and walk right back into Braden's hands?

We would head north, Dr. Favor said. And keep heading north. The McLaren girl said she agreed, but which way was it? He pointed off somewhere, but you could tell he wasn't sure. Or he could go on alone, Dr. Favor suggested, watching us to see our reaction. Go on alone and bring back help. He didn't insist on it and let it die when nobody said anything.

Why didn't he mention his wife then? That's when I started thinking about what the McLaren girl had said earlier: that he had forgotten about his wife and only the money was important to him.

Could that be? I tried thinking what I would do if it was my wife. Hole up and ambush them? Try and get her away from them? My gosh, no, I thought then. Just trade them the money for her! Certainly Dr. Favor must have thought of that.

Then why didn't he do it? Or at least talk about it. When you got down to it, though, it was his business. I mean we had no right to remind him of what he should do. That was his business. I don't mean to sound hard or callous; that's just the way it was. We had enough on our minds without worrying about his wife.

We just sat there until Dr. Favor said he was going. When he started off, the McLaren girl started after him, so Mendez and I did too. I guess we had to follow somebody.

From then on I don't know where we were or even what direction we went.

By then there wasn't much talk among us. Once in a while Dr. Favor said something, usually about what way to go. One time though he brought up the subject again of us hiding somewhere and him going on alone.

Mendez said it was all right with him, not caring one way or the other. But neither the McLaren girl nor I would agree to it. I kept picturing Braden somewhere behind us waiting for morning so he could get on our sign and run us down. Who would want to just sit there waiting for him?

The McLaren girl looked at it another way. She said right to Dr. Favor's face, "That money's been stolen enough. Don't worry about one of us trying to take it."

"As if I'd distrust you people," Dr. Favor said. "The things you think about."

"I'd like to know what you think about," the McLaren girl said. "Since it sure isn't your wife."

Dr. Favor didn't say anything and we went on.

If you were to ask me who was the best one, who took it the best and never once complained, who even walked with hardly any trouble, I would say the McLaren girl. If you are surprised, remember she had been held by wild Apaches over a month. She had traveled with them as they kept on the move, keeping up with them else they would have killed her. You looked at her and wondered how something like that could have happened to a young girl and still not see it on her face.

Once she offered to take the grainsack or blanket roll I was carrying, but I wouldn't hear of it.

She even said we should still keep going when finally Dr. Favor led us off into a gully and announced we would camp there. He said if we stopped now we would have a better chance of finding Russell when daylight came. I'm not sure what he meant by that and think it was just an excuse, the real reason for his wanting to stop being his tiredness. The McLaren girl argued we should use the darkness while we had it—it was still a few hours before sunup—but gave in when she saw how tired Mendez was. So tired he could hardly stand up.

We had already eaten some of the biscuits and dried meat from the grainsack. Now there was nothing to do but sleep. I was the only one with a blanket, so I offered it to the McLaren girl. She said no, for me to use it. I did, finally, but all rolled up as a pillow. (Somebody might think this was dumb, but I couldn't cover myself with it being the only one. It would have felt good too, I can tell you that.)

It was only a few hours before sunup when we stopped here; so there wasn't much time to sleep, and it was hard getting to sleep, even as tired as I felt. But finally I did.

In the morning there weren't two words said by anyone. You know how it can be in the morning anyway: on top of having slept no more than two and a half hours on the ground and in the cold after walking almost all night. (Yes, it was cold. Even though during the day it was blistering hot.) And on top of that not knowing where you were and Braden coming after us on horseback.

The only thing we were sure of in the morning was the direction north and that was the way we went, having eaten a little more of the dried beef and biscuits and taken a few swallows of water each.

Going toward the north does not mean we went in a straight line. Unless you wanted to climb steep slopes all the time, and maybe get up there and find no way down, you had to follow the washes and draws that cut through this high country, so that maybe you would walk two, even three miles to get one mile north. You can see nobody talked much. That's the way it was all morning, or until the next part happened which I would judge was an hour or so before noon.

We came out of some trees onto an open meadow, a little graze like that was cupped there in the hills, then crossing the meadow and taking the only way out, we went up a pretty long draw that was deep and lined with thick brush and rocks along both sides, the draw being about sixty feet wide and upwards to three hundred or more feet long, that being a calculation from memory.

We made our way up this draw, looking back across the meadow as we went, finally reached the top and almost dropped everything we carried. Not out of tiredness, out of surprise!

For sitting there with his Spencer across his lap and smoking a cigarette was John Russell.

Mendez yelled his name and ran over to him, Mendez assuming just as I did, I guess, that Russell had changed his mind and gotten the mean feeling out of his system, and now wanted to show us the way out of here.

Mendez scolded him a little, but in a kidding way, that he shouldn't have done what he did. Mendez was too glad to see Russell to be serious or angry at him, telling him how we couldn't keep up with him and how worn out we got trying to.

Russell moved him aside with his arm and motioned all of us back from the crest so we wouldn't be seen from below.

From the way Mendez acted, our troubles were over.

Not so according to Dr. Favor. He said, staring at Russell, "You going to sit there for a while, are you?"

Russell didn't move. "You want to go bad, uh?"

He saw that Russell had no intention of getting up. "Now it comes," Dr. Favor said. "I want to hear how you'll say this."

"You want to go," Russell said, "go on."

Dr. Favor kept looking at him. "What else?"

"Leave the saddlebag and the gun here."

Dr. Favor's big red face almost seemed to relax and smile. "There," he said. "Right out in the open. It took you all night to realize you'd run off and left something behind."

Mendez, not understanding, had that worried look again. "What is it?" he said to Russell.

"It's my money," Dr. Favor said. "He's thinking it looks pretty good. Out here and no law to stop him. But four people against one. Maybe he hasn't thought about that."

Russell drew on the cigarette. "Maybe one is enough," he said.

That was when the McLaren girl stepped in. "Your money," she yelled at Dr. Favor. I mean *yelled* it. "After you stole it! We're supposed to side with you to protect money you stole!" Then her eyes took in Russell too. "You sit here arguing about money and giving Frank Braden all the time he'd ever need."

"Be careful what you say," Dr. Favor said to her. "I think you are talking without thinking. This is my money, in my possession, and it will take more than the word of a dead outlaw to prove it isn't."

"All this talk," Mendez said, like he had just thought of it. "We have to *move*."

Russell looked up at him. "Where do you want to go?"

Mendez said, "Are you crazy? They're coming!"

"Tell me where," Russell said.

"Where? I don't know. Out of here."

"I'll tell you something," Russell said. "There's open country. Maybe it takes you two, three hours to cross it. And while you're there they come with their horses."

"Then hide somewhere," Mendez said, "and wait for dark to cross it."

Russell nodded. "Or do better than that. Wait for them here. Shoot their horses to make it even, uh? Maybe finish it."

"Finish it," I said, understanding him, but I guess not believing what he was asking us to do. "You mean try and kill them?"

"If they get close enough," Russell said, "they're going to kill you."

"But they didn't harm anybody before. Why would they want to now?"

"Do you want to give them your water?"

"They got water."

"Two canteens which they were drinking out of all day yesterday. Do you want to give them yours?"

"No, but—"

"Then they'll kill you for it."

Until then it seemed just a matter of running and getting away or running and being caught and they getting the money after all. But kill them or they would kill us? It was a terrible thing to think about and you couldn't help looking for other ways. Run or hide. Run or hide. Those ways kept popping into your head while Russell just sat there looking down the draw and waiting.

"And if we don't *finish it*," Dr. Favor said, making those last words sound dumb to have ever been thought of. "What then?"

"You don't have a say in this," Russell said, looking up at him. "You can stay or go, but either way you leave the saddlebag."

"You must have kept awake all night," Dr. Favor said.

"It came to me," Russell said back.

"How much you figure I have?"

Russell shrugged. "It doesn't matter."

"Wouldn't take much, would it, to keep you in whisky?"

"You leave the belly gun too," Russell said. And held out his hand for it, turning just a little so that the Spencer in his lap turned with him.

Dr. Favor just stared, not moving. "You're forgetting something," he said. "What if the others decide against you?"

"Then they have you to lead them," Russell answered.

He sat there with his hand still held toward Dr. Favor and you knew he could sit there the rest of his life and never budge. It was his way if we stayed with him. It was either do what he wanted or else go on with Dr. Favor. It was not like choosing between a good thing or a bad thing. Still, one felt to be better than the other and it wasn't much of a hard choice to make.

The McLaren girl was the one who said it out loud, though not very loud. "I would like to go home," she said, hardly glancing at Dr. Favor. "I sure would like to go home. And I know he can't find the way."

Neither Mendez nor I had to say anything. If we'd sided with Dr. Favor, we would have.

With us watching him, I believe, Dr. Favor didn't want to get caught looking awkward or nervous. You had to give him credit for that. He took it calmly, not offering any argument, but I will bet thinking fast all the time. He just shrugged and handed his revolver to Russell.

"Chief make plenty war now," he said. You see how he was passing it off? Like Russell was a bully you had to give in to if you wanted some peace.

Russell didn't pay any attention. He took the gun, then looked at Mendez, noticing Mendez had Lamarr Dean's revolver besides his shotgun.

"You shoot all right?" he asked.

Mendez frowned. "I'm not sure."

"You'll find out," Russell said. "First the shotgun. When they're close. So close you can touch them. Then the other one if you need it."

"I don't know," Mendez said, worried. "Just sit and wait for them like that."

"If there was a better way," Russell said, "we would do it." Just that moment talking to Mendez, Russell's voice was gentle and you remembered they had known each other before and maybe had been friends.

He looked off down the draw, studying the trees over the other side of the meadow. If they were on our sign, he knew, they would come through there and up the draw.

Then he was looking right at me and handing me Dr. Favor's revolver. At first I didn't make any move to take it.

He pushed it out again like telling me, "Come on, take it," and that time I did.

"You have one thing to do," he said and shifted his eyes over to Dr. Favor and back again. "Watch him."

Then it was the McLaren girl's turn. She stood there, her dark nice-looking face very calm, seeing Russell looking at her then.

"You stay with this one," Russell said, meaning me.

"Carl Allen," the McLaren girl said.

It stopped Russell just for a second as if she'd interrupted his thoughts. "You'll have the saddlebag and the water."

"Squaw work," Dr. Favor said. "You ought to like that." He was also saying, "See what you're getting yourself in for?"

It didn't bother her, or else she was so intent on Russell she didn't hear him. She said, "The money and the waterskin, but you carry your own water I see." She meant the canteen that was on the ground next to him. The one he and Mendez had used.

He watched her, getting all the meaning out of her words that she didn't say. "You want it too?"

"Why burden yourself?" she said, and you weren't sure if she was serious or not.

For just a moment there John Russell hesitated, as if handing over the canteen would be giving up his independence. But he did and the McLaren girl took it.

"You and you and you," Russell said, meaning the McLaren girl and Dr. Favor and I, "will be here. You don't stand up. You don't move back away from the edge here and stand up. You sit and don't move." (Like a teacher talking to little children in school!) "Him—"

"Reverend Dr. Favor," the McLaren girl said with that little knife edge in her voice again.

"He can leave up to the time they come," Russell went on. "After that, no." Russell was looking right at me again, but still talking about Dr. Favor.

"If he tries to leave with nothing, shoot him once," Russell said. "If he takes the saddlebag, shoot him twice. If he picks up the water, empty your gun. You understand that?"

(I have thought about those words since then and I am sure Russell was having a little fun with us when he said that. Part serious, part in fun. But can you imagine joking at a time like that? That of course was the reason no one even smiled. He must have thought we were dumb.)

I just nodded, not wanting to say anything with Dr. Favor standing right there.

"I don't know," Mendez said. You could see what had been going on in his mind. "Maybe we should just keep going, try and outrun them."

"You run now," Russell said to him, "they'll catch you and kill you. Believe that more than you believe anything."

Russell told us again to stay where we were, down low. He talked to Mendez, going over it again with him, telling him to wait till they got close and to be sure of hitting something, to shoot first at the men, then at the horses; but watch for the woman. Mendez listened, nodding sometimes, but kept looking over toward us.

After that Russell didn't waste any more talk. He and Mendez crawled out through the brush, working their way about forty feet down the draw, then separating, Mendez staying on the right, Russell crawling way over to the left side so that anybody coming up the draw would pass between them. If one did not have a good shot when the time came, the other probably would.

Both had good cover, for there were sizable rocks that had been washed down the draw, mostly along the sides where they were, and pretty thick brush where there weren't any rocks. Only the middle ground, where water would run off in the spring, was fairly open.

Russell had this timed pretty well, knowing how long it would take them to get on our sign and follow us. He had figured a few other things too. That they wouldn't be as careful by now as they had been yesterday evening and during the first hour or so this morning. There had been good ambush places before this, but nothing had jumped out at them. Why should it now? They would be awake, of course, wide awake coming up something like this draw; but they would tend to keep their eyes on the top and expect it to come from there if it was coming at all.

(It is easy to talk about something like this. It is also interesting to plan and imagine what you would do, but only as long as you aren't there. I wouldn't sit where we were, just waiting there again, no matter what anybody gave me.)

We kept our eyes on the trees that were some kind of pine, big ones, probably ponderosa, across the meadow at the bottom of the draw. Still, when they came, it wasn't sudden at all.

Right at the edge of the trees, in shadow, was a horse and rider and you wondered how long he had been there with you looking right at him. He was awake all right.

He came out of the trees holding to a slow walk

and was out in the meadow a ways before the next rider appeared. Then another one came who you knew right away was the Favor woman. (I did not look over at Dr. Favor to see what his face showed. I would have if I had known I was going to write this.) The fourth one was right behind her. That would be Frank Braden, the big sugar of this outfit. He would be the one telling the others what to do, while he stayed with their hostage or whatever Mrs. Favor was.

It was the Mexican rider who dismounted and came first when they reached the bottom of the draw. He seemed to be making sure of our tracks, walking along a little ways with his head down. Then he swung back up and he and Early came on, the Mexican staying a little bit in the lead. They kept looking up at the sides of the draw, being very watchful now. They knew we had come this way and I think they smelled it as a fresh trail. Not so much Early as the Mexican.

You got the feeling he knew by the sign that Russell had passed through here on his own or ahead of us, or maybe Russell had left no tracks at all and the Mexican saw only that the four of us had come up this way. There is nothing to prove this, but I believe he did know. The Mexican seemed so sure of himself, riding right up the middle of the draw first, seeming relaxed but his eyes taking everything in.

Braden, with the Favor woman, kept a good ten lengths back of Early and the Mexican. That was the way they came up, walking right into it.

It was like watching a play. No, it was realer than that. (My gosh, it couldn't get more real!) It gave you a strange feeling to watch it, thinking that in a minute or two you were going to see somebody get killed.

Russell never moved. We could see just part of him. He lay full length as if asleep. His hat was off and his head was down, as if he was listening to them coming up the draw instead of watching them.

Mendez kept looking over to where Russell was, but I doubt he could see him, being on about the same level. Then he would look back up in our direction. You could see he wanted no part of this. Why couldn't he be up where we were? Or the rest of us down there helping him, he was probably thinking. Mendez was nervous. You couldn't blame him for it. Still, it was strange to see him in that state. (In the last two days I had certainly learned a lot about show-nothing, tell-nothing Henry Mendez.)

As Early and the Mexican got up a ways, they started looking up at the top of the draw and studying it. Especially the Mexican. He was closer to Mendez's side of the draw now and about five horselengths ahead of Early. Halfway up, the Mexican drew his right-hand gun and held it ready.

You saw Mendez pressing himself tight against the rock he was behind and not looking around now. He would inch up to sneak a look at the Mexican and then duck down again. You almost knew what he was thinking. You also knew this wasn't something he had done before.

Looking at Russell you couldn't even tell if he was alive, laying there sighting down his carbine now and waiting as if he could wait like that all day, waiting for Early to ride right up to him.

I don't remember what the McLaren girl and Dr. Favor were doing then. I could feel them there. The thing is, the one I really wanted to watch was Russell; then you would see how this was done. But Mendez, the way he was fidgeting, looking up at the Mexican coming and then pressing against the rock, made you nervous and you kept watching him, holding your breath for fear he was going to jump up and start running.

The Mexican was now about a hundred feet away from him, sitting round-shouldered and relaxed, the Colt gun held about chest high and pointed straight up, the sun glinting and moving a little with the motion of the horse and rider.

That was what Mendez saw coming toward him, a man holding a gun that seemed part of his hand, and another gun still holstered; a man you knew was ready, but could still be relaxed about it and not sit stiff in the saddle or with his shoulders hunched.

Maybe if I was Mendez I would have done the same as he did. Which was all of a sudden rise up and fire both barrels of that scatter gun like he couldn't let go fast enough.

At a hundred feet or less, some of the buckshot could have found the Mexican, but Mendez hurried and didn't aim at all. The Mexican straightened and fired three times, faster than I've ever seen a man thumb and fire a Colt revolver, with all three shots zinging off the rocks Mendez had flattened himself behind. Then you saw the Mexican twist in the saddle, like something had pushed him, and grab his side right above the belt.

Russell had fired.

He fired again as the Mexican rolled out of the saddle and into cover. He fired again and the Mexican's horse threw up its head, shaking it, and sunk on its forelegs and fell over.

Early was already off and in cover. You saw him reach up to grab his horse's reins as it reared around and started off down the draw. Early missed. Russell didn't though. He fired twice again, quick, and I swear you heard both shots smack into that horse. The horse went down, rolled on its side and got up again and kept going, following Braden and the Favor woman—Braden holding her horse's reins close at the bit ring and leading it as they rode back down the draw, all the way down to the bottom and around the outcrop of rocks into a little patch of scrubby woods. Even after they were out of sight you heard the horses in the thicket. Then everything was quiet.

It was quiet for the longest time. Mendez kept looking over to about where Russell was, not knowing at all what to do and maybe expecting some signal from him.

Russell didn't move. You could see he had learned a lot from the Apaches, a kind of patience few white men could ever command. He lay there sighting, I think, on the place where Early had gone into the brush, waiting for a movement. He lay like that, I swear, for about two hours, all the while this stand-off lasted.

Not much happened during that time. The Mexican started calling out either to Russell or Mendez in Spanish. I didn't know what he was saying, but they were questions, and there was a sound to his voice like the questions were meant to be funny. Not funny, exactly, but like insults or inviting Mendez to step out and show himself, things you wouldn't expect to hear coming out of that draw. You had to give that Mexican something. There was no doubt he had been shot. Still he could yell at Russell and Mendez, trying to draw them out.

Once there was a quick glimpse of Early. He was there and then gone, off behind a scatter of rocks a little farther down the draw. Russell must have been waiting for the Mexican because he didn't fire. We never did see the Mexican squirm out of there and Early only that one time.

Both of them worked their way down though. They stood out in the open for a second, way down at the bottom of the draw. The Mexican, holding his side with one hand, waved to us. Then they were gone into the thicket.

Just for a few minutes we had time to rest, not wondering where they were or worrying about them coming. They would have to think things over and maybe wait until dark to come up that draw again. Though we couldn't count on it. We couldn't sit here for long either. One of them could circle around, even though it would take time, and we wouldn't ever be able to move.

So we had to get out of there. When Russell and Mendez came up, I opened the canteen. Nobody had had any water since this morning. But Russell shook his head. "Tonight," he said. "Not while the sun is out." Meaning, I guess, you would sweat it out right away and be thirsty again before you knew it.

That was all he said, with not one word to Mendez about shooting too soon and spoiling the ambush. That was over as far as he was concerned; he was not the kind of man who would stew over something finished and past fixing. He just picked up his blanket roll and that meant it was time to go.

Maybe we had showed them it wasn't going to be easy, as Russell had said we might. But look at it another way. We might have finished it in the draw, but we didn't and maybe never would. The only good to come out of the ambush was now they had one less horse—maybe two.

But now they were close. Now they knew where we were. And now there was no doubt they would come with guns out and shoot on sight.

4

We sat there only a few minutes. That's all the longer our rest time lasted, and it was starting again. Only not the way we expected it to. We didn't go right then. We were about to when the McLaren girl said, "Look—" pointing down the draw.

We looked, but we all crouched down at the same time. There, way down at the bottom, was the Mexican again, his straw hat bright in the sunlight so that you knew it was the Mexican and not one of the others. But we could not tell at first what he was carrying. He had to get up a ways— taking his time, his face raised, his one hand holding his side—before we saw it was a stick with something white tied to the end of it.

He seemed careful, but not scared, keeping his eyes on the ridge, not sure we would honor his white truce flag, I guess, and ready to dive for cover if we let go at him. He was armed with both his revolvers.

Nobody said anything. We just watched. He kept coming, almost reaching the place where Mendez had been during the ambush.

Russell stood up holding his carbine in one hand, pointed down, and the Mexican stopped.

Russell said, "You come to give up?"

The Mexican stood at ease, letting his truce flag dip down to the ground. I think he smiled when Russell said that, but I'm not sure.

I know he shook his head. He said, "When you learn to shoot better." He raised his hand from his side and there was blood on it.

"You didn't do so good."

"I tried to do better," Russell said. "I think you moved."

"Moved," the Mexican said. "How do you like them, tied to a tree?"

"On a horse," Russell said. "Like your friend."

The Mexican grinned. "You like to pull the trigger."

"I can do it again for you," Russell said.

"You could," the Mexican agreed, staring up at Russell, studying him and judging the distance between them. "I have to talk to this other one first. This Favor."

He pronounced it Fa-*vor*, like it was a Spanish word.

"He can hear you," Russell said.

"If he can't you tell him," the Mexican said. "This. He gives us the money . . . and some of the water. We give him his wife and everyone goes home. Ask him how he likes that."

"You're out of water?"

"Almost." The Mexican grinned. "That Early. He put whisky in his canteen. He thought it would be easy."

Russell shook his head. "It will get even harder."

"Not if this Fa*vor* gives us the money."

"He doesn't have it," Russell said.

The Mexican grinned again. "Tell me he hid it."

Russell shook his head. "He gave it to me."

The Mexican nodded, looking up at Russell like he was admiring him. "So now you steal the money." He shrugged his shoulders. "All right, we trade with you then."

"She's not my woman," Russell said.

"We give her to you."

"What else?"

"Your life. How's that?"

"Tell Braden how things are now," Russell said.

"What's the difference who has the money?" the Mexican said. "You give it to us or we shoot that woman."

"All right," Russell said. "You shoot her."

The Mexican kept staring at him. "What about the rest of them? What do they say?"

"They say what they want," Russell said. "I say what I want. Do you see that now?"

He didn't see it. He didn't know what to think,

so he just stood there, one hand on his side, the other holding that truce flag.

"Tell Braden how it is," Russell said. "Tell him to think some more."

"He'll say the same thing."

"Tell him anyway."

The Mexican hadn't taken his eyes off Russell for a second, sizing him up all the while they talked. "Maybe you and I finish something first," he said. "Maybe you come down here a little."

"I'm thinking," Russell said, "whether to kill you right now or wait till you turn around."

Do you know what the Mexican did? He smiled. Not that unbelieving kind of smile, but like he appreciated Russell or enjoyed him. It was about the strangest thing I ever saw. He smiled and said, "If I didn't believe you, I think you would do it. All right, I talk to Braden."

He turned and walked away dragging the truce flag, not with his shoulders hunched like he expected something, but as calmly as he had walked up.

Russell waited until the Mexican was almost down to the bottom. He got his blanket roll and the saddlebags, just glanced at us, and moved off. He didn't tell us what he had planned. If we wanted to follow him that was up to us.

We didn't expect this. We thought he would talk to them again. But who could be sure what Russell was thinking? We knew we couldn't sit in that draw forever. Sooner or later Braden would try to get at us. But was going on right then the best way? Russell must have thought so, though he wasn't telling us why.

We followed him. What choice had we?

That was a funny thing. I felt closer to Dr. Favor than I did to Russell. Dr. Favor might have stolen government money and left his wife to her own fate; but it was something you had to think about before you realized it. He never admitted either right out.

Russell was something else. He had said to the Mexican, not caring who heard him, "All right, shoot her." Like she was nothing to him, so what did he care? Do you see the difference? Russell was so cold and calm about it, it scared you to death. Also, if he didn't care about her, what did he care about us?

Now it was almost like the whole thing was between Braden and Russell and we were in it only because there wasn't any place else to go. Like it was all Russell's fault and he had dragged us into it.

I would say we walked three miles from the time we left that draw until we stopped again, though we did not gain more than one mile in actual distance. We kept pretty much to ridges, high up as possible in the cover of pinyon pine and scrub, and when we stopped it was because flat country opened up at the end of the canyon not far ahead of us. It was a good two or three miles across the openness before the hills took up again.

Russell didn't say it and nobody asked, but we knew he planned to wait for dark to cross that open part. It was no place to be seen in daylight by three men riding horses. (We did not know then whether Russell had killed one or two of their horses.)

We had climbed a pretty steep grade to reach this place we camped at (high up the way Apaches always camp, whether there is water or not) with thick pinyon on three sides of us and the slope, with some cliffrose and scrub, on the open side.

Russell had made it hard for them to follow. If they came directly on our sign, they would have to come up the open slope. If they came any other way, it would take them hours to work around, and then they would be taking a chance of not finding us. So, we figured, they would come directly when they came. All right, but to come up that open slope they would have to wait until dark. Which was what we would be waiting for to slip off through the trees.

Do you see how Russell figured to stay one jump ahead of them? I estimated we would reach the old San Pete mine some time during the night; Delgado's if we were lucky, some time during the next afternoon or evening. Then home. It didn't seem far when you looked ahead. The trouble was you had to keep looking back.

After the little sleep we had had it was good to lie down again. Everybody picked out a spot. We couldn't make a fire so we ate some more of the biscuits, which were pretty hard by now, and the dried strip meat which never was very good.

We did not drink any water though. John Russell had said we would have to wait until night. It was midafternoon now. Imagine not having had a drink since that morning. The salty beef didn't help your thirst any either. But what could we do?

I kept picturing myself sitting on a shady porch with a big pitcher of ice water, sitting there in a clean shirt having just shaved and taken a bath. Boy!

Mendez looked ten years older, his eyes sunken in and his face covered with beard stubble. Dr. Favor's big, broad face, framed by that half-moon-shaped beard, was sweaty looking. The McLaren girl and John Russell were the only ones who didn't look so bad, I mean not as dirty or sweaty as the rest of us. With her hair too short to muss and her dark skin, she looked like she was taking it all right. John Russell was dusty, of course, but had no beard to make his face look dirty. You could tell he had pulled out the stubbles Indian-fashion when he first started to get a beard, years ago, and now he'd never have one.

Russell stayed mostly by the open side, lying down but propped on his elbows and looking down the way we had come up. I guess he was resting and doing his thinking now, taking time to see things clearly. Whatever he saw in his mind, it got him up on his feet after a while.

He brought the saddlebags over to me and dropped them. He didn't say guard them, but that's what his look meant. All he said was he would go have a look at things and he left, taking only the Spencer carbine; no water or anything else. He didn't go straight down the slope but headed off through the pinyon, I guess to keep high up as he scouted the ground we had covered from the draw.

A little while after he was gone, Dr. Favor went over to where the waterskin and canteen and provisions were. He picked up the canteen and was drinking from it before anyone had time to yell stop. It was the McLaren girl who yelled it.

She jumped up, and Dr. Favor held the canteen out to her. "Your turn," he said.

"We're not to drink till tonight. You know that."

"I forget," Dr. Favor said. She could believe him or not; he didn't care.

Mendez, still sitting down, said, "Maybe we should all take one, to keep it even."

"To keep it even!" the McLaren girl said. "What

about later when we don't have any. What good does keeping it even do?"

"I'm thinking of now," Mendez said, rising. "You can think of any time you want."

"All right," the girl said. "And what about Russell?"

"Look"—Mendez had this surprised sound to his voice—"if he wants to wait till dark, all right. That's up to him. We drink when we want."

"He doesn't even have to know," Dr. Favor said. He saw Mendez liked this idea so he put it out there again. "If you're worried about Russell, why would he even have to know?"

"And you think that would be fair," the McLaren girl said.

"It's his rule," Dr. Favor said. "If it's unfair, he brought it on himself."

"Look," Mendez said, making it sound simple, "if you want to wait, you wait. If you want a drink now, then you take it."

That was when he grabbed the canteen from Dr. Favor and took a good drink, more even than Favor had, so that Dr. Favor reached for it and pulled it out of Mendez's mouth.

"You said keep it even."

Then he handed the canteen to the McLaren girl.

She took it, her eyes right on Dr. Favor and hesitating just a little before she put it to her mouth. If this surprises you, look at it this way: they could drink it all while you sat there obeying Russell's rule. All right, if they were going to have some, a person would be dumb not to take his share. That's why I took a drink right after she did. I'm sure she was thinking the same way.

Dr. Favor was still looking at her, more sure of himself than ever now. He said, "If you want to tell him when he gets back, you just go right ahead." He was even smiling then.

What could she say? On the other hand, knowing her, she might have said something at that. But she didn't.

Everybody settled down again. For a little while there was peace. Then Dr. Favor came over to me.

Right away he said, "That's some Indian chief we got," meaning Russell of course.

"Well," I said, "I guess he knows what he's doing."

"He knows what he wants. That much is sure."

If he thought Russell wanted the money, that was his business. But why talk about something you couldn't prove? I just said, "Maybe he's the best chief we got," kind of joking about it.

"Only we're not his braves," Dr. Favor said, and he was serious, his face close to mine and staring right at me.

"If somebody has another idea," I said, "I'll listen."

"I've got one," he said. "We leave right now."

He'd force you right up against a wall like that; then you'd have to try and wiggle out.

"Well, I don't know about that," I said.

"Let me have my gun then."

He said it all of a sudden and I didn't have any idea in the world what to say back. What I finally said was something like, "Well, I don't think I can do that."

"Because he said so?"

"No, not just because of him."

"Because of the others?"

"We're all in this together."

"But not going by his rules anymore."

"Just the water."

"What's more important than that?"

"I'm holding it," I said. "He's the one took it."

"Now that doesn't make much sense, does it?" Dr. Favor said. "What you're doing, you're keeping something that doesn't belong to you."

I couldn't tell the man to his face I thought he was a thief. That's why I had so much trouble thinking of something to say. Even with the gun in my belt, or maybe because it was there, I felt awkward and dumb. He just kept staring at me.

"Maybe I should take it away from you," he said.

When I hesitated, not knowing what to say or

do, the McLaren girl got into it. She said, looking at me, "Are you going to let him?"

She pushed up to a sitting position, about ten or twelve feet away from us. "You know what he wants," she said.

"What's mine," Dr. Favor said. "If you think anything else, you're imagining things."

"I know one thing," the McLaren girl said. "I wouldn't give you the gun if I had it. And if you tried to take it, I'd shoot you."

"For hardly more than a little girl," Dr. Favor said, "you certainly have strong opinions."

"When I know I'm right," the McLaren girl said.

Dr. Favor stood up. He lit a cigar and for a while stood there looking out over the slope and smoking. Time crept along. I laid down with one arm on the saddlebags and my head on my arm. I don't think I have ever been so tired, and it was easy to close my eyes and fall asleep. I fought it for a while, dozing, opening my eyes. Once when I opened them, I saw Dr. Favor sitting by Mendez and Mendez was smoking a cigar too.

I heard Dr. Favor say, "You did fine. It took more nerve than most have to lie there waiting for them."

"He shouldn't have made me do it," Mendez said.

"You didn't have to, you know."

"Listen, he makes sense," Mendez said. "Whether you agree with him or not."

"He makes sense even if it kills you," Dr. Favor said. "That's what you're saying."

"It's just I had never shot at a man before," Mendez said. "It isn't an easy thing."

"It seems easy to him," Dr. Favor said. "And if you can kill one person, you can kill four."

"For what reason?"

"My money," Dr. Favor said.

Mendez shook his head. "I know him better than that."

"Where money is concerned," Dr. Favor said, "you don't know anybody."

Within the next quarter of an hour Dr. Favor proved those words.

I should have taken them as a warning, but I had not for a minute thought he would ever use force. By the time I woke up (I mean actually woke up, for I had dozed off again) it was too late. Dr. Favor was standing over me with Mendez's shotgun pointed right at my head.

Mendez sat there with his legs crossed and his shoulders hunched as if he didn't care what was happening—as if Dr. Favor had just taken the gun and Mendez hadn't lifted an eyebrow to stop him.

The McLaren girl was watching too. She had been lying on her side, but now pushed herself up on one arm as Dr. Favor took the revolver from me first and then the saddlebags. He went over to the waterskin next and filled up the two-quart canteen from it, leaving hardly anything in the skin.

That's when the McLaren girl finally spoke. She said, "Maybe you'll leave us your blessing since you're taking everything else."

Dr. Favor was past arguing with anybody. He didn't say a word. He opened the canvas grain-sack, looked at the meat and biscuits inside like he was going to take some out, but he pulled the neck closed and swung it over his shoulder with the saddlebags.

He was standing like that, ready to move off, when John Russell appeared out of the pinyon.

They stood facing each other about twenty feet apart, Russell holding the Spencer against his leg and pointed down; Favor holding the sawed-off shotgun the same way.

"You got everything?" Russell said.

"What's mine," Favor answered.

"You better put it down," Russell said. It sounded like he meant the shotgun.

Mendez must have felt funny about Dr. Favor holding it. He said, "He just took it. I closed my eyes and he had it."

Dr. Favor shook his head slowly. "Like I'm against everybody. Like I was running off on my own."

"You sure had us fooled then," the McLaren girl said, her voice dry and sharp enough to pierce right through him.

"Believe what you like," Dr. Favor said. "I was going to get help. One man can travel faster than five. With food and water he could make it out of here in no time and have help back in less than a day."

"So you elected yourself," the McLaren girl said.

"I've tried to reason with you people before," Dr. Favor said. "I decided it was time to do something besides waste my breath."

Russell's eyes never left Dr. Favor. "Put it down or else use it," he said. "You have two ways to go." His tone seemed to say he didn't care which Favor did. One way would be as easy as the other.

"There's no talking to a man who relies only on force," Dr. Favor said. He shrugged, hesitating, holding on by his fingernails for a moment, waiting for Russell to drop his guard for one second. Maybe he could beat Russell, he was probably thinking. But if he didn't beat him, he would be dead. If he tied Russell, he could also be dead.

Maybe that was the way he thought and he didn't like the odds. Maybe if he gave in now he would get a better chance later on. I guess he knew nobody believed his story about getting help, but he didn't care what we thought. Whatever he was thinking, it told him today wasn't the day. He let the shotgun and revolver fall, then lifted off the grainsack and saddlebags.

No, it didn't bother him at all what we thought. He turned his back on us and strolled over by the cliffrose bushes to look down the grade. As if telling us he knew we wouldn't do anything to him, so what did he care what we thought?

But that's where he was wrong. John Russell did not just think things.

As Dr. Favor stood there, Russell said, "Keep going."

All we saw was his back for a minute. Dr. Favor seemed to be waiting for the rest of it: "—if you ever try that again." Or "—if you don't behave yourself." You know.

But there wasn't any rest of it. Russell had said it all.

When Dr. Favor realized this, he turned around to look at Russell. His face had lost a little of its calm cocksureness. Not all, just some. But maybe at that point he half believed Russell might be bluffing.

Maybe, he thought, if he could just pass a little time it would blow over.

He said, "You're betting my money I won't survive all alone."

"You could do it," Russell said. "With some luck."

"If I don't, it's the same as murder."

"Like the way you killed those people at San Carlos."

"This is a new one," Dr. Favor said. "First I'm accused of stealing my own money. Now murder."

"Without enough to eat," Russell said, "people sicken and die. I saw that at Whiteriver and also I heard things, how the agent had money to buy more beef, but he had a way of keeping the money to himself."

"A way," Dr. Favor said. "You figure the way and then prove it."

"That one called Dean said enough."

Dr. Favor seemed to smile. "But you went and killed our witness."

"You think I need one?" Russell said.

We weren't in any court. We were fifty miles out in high desert country, and John Russell was standing there with a .56-56 Spencer in his hand. All he had to do was raise it and Dr. Favor was gone forever.

There wasn't any question, Dr. Favor knew it.

It is hard to try and imagine what was going on in his mind then, because I never did learn much about this Dr. Alexander Favor.

Look at him for a minute. A heavyset man, both in his body and in his opinion of himself. He did what he wanted and did not take much pushing from others. He had been Indian Agent at San Carlos about two years, having come from somewhere in Ohio. The "Doctor" part of his name was not medicine. I have learned that he was a Doctor of the Faith Reform Church. But I had never heard him preaching anything, so you cannot accuse him of not practicing it.

Evidently he got into that profession to make money and for that reason only, thinking it would be an easy way: the same reason he applied to the government to become an Indian Agent and got sent to San Carlos. Though he could have just made up the divinity title and got the appointment through some friend in the Interior Department. I would not like to think that he had ever honestly been a preacher.

He must have started withholding government funds soon after he got to San Carlos to build up the amount in the saddlebags. About twelve thousand dollars. He probably made some of it off supply contractors who paid him in order to get the government business. So you know one thing for sure; he was dishonest. A thief no matter what he hid behind.

You can also say he was a man who cared more about his money than his wife. But maybe he always did. I mean maybe she was just a woman to him. Someone to have around, but not feeling about her the way most men felt about their wives. I mean liking them along with having them there.

Maybe he did like her, but she never liked him and didn't care if he knew it. I think that is the way it was, judging from the way she didn't pay any attention to him on the stagecoach and fooled with Frank Braden right in front of him. I think even then Dr. Favor had finally had enough of her. Leaving her was a good way to pay her back.

You knew good and well he wasn't thinking about her right now. I doubt he was even thinking about the money. Right now he just had his life to worry about. Russell wasn't letting him take anything else.

There was that little space of silence where he must have been digging in his mind to say something more to Russell, to scare him or put him in his place or something. But he must have thought what was the use? Why waste breath?

He looked at Mendez though, then at the McLaren girl and said, "You take care of yourselves now. Do everything he tells you." He was turning then to go. "And remember, don't drink any water till tonight."

We watched him step through the cliffrose bushes and he was gone. Russell went over to the edge, but the McLaren girl and Mendez and I didn't move. Not for a moment anyway. Maybe we were afraid Favor would look back up and see us watching him and laugh or say something else about the water.

When I walked over finally and looked down the grade, he was past the steepest part but having an awful time, skidding and raising dust all the way. We watched him down at the bottom, standing there for a minute, looking up canyon to the flat country that opened up there. He crossed the canyon to the other side and started up a little wash (he had learned something from Russell) and after a minute you couldn't see him for the brush and the steepness of the cutbank.

Nobody said a word.

Without Russell I know we could never have sat there in that place until dark. It was too easy to imagine them sneaking up on you, knowing they were out there somewhere and drawing closer all the time. Russell sat watching the slope. Then he'd move off into the trees for a time. He never said anything. He smoked a little, maybe twice. Most of the time though he sat watching; watching and I think listening. But all that time there was no sign of them.

As it started to get dark in the trees, we ate again and Russell held up the canteen and handed it to the McLaren girl.

"Finally, uh?" he said.

She didn't look at him. She took a drink and passed the canteen to me. Mendez was next. Then Russell took his turn. The McLaren girl watched him drink, holding the water in his mouth before swallowing it, and I kept thinking: She's going to tell him.

Russell lowered the canteen.

Now, I thought, waiting for her to speak.

Russell pushed the cork in tight. She watched him. I think right then she almost told, so near to doing it the words were formed in her mouth. But she didn't say it.

She said instead, "Maybe we should have let him take some." Meaning Dr. Favor.

Russell looked at her.

"I mean just some," the McLaren girl said.

I thought of something then. All of a sudden. "We left a waterskin at the San Pete! Remember that?"

The McLaren girl looked at me. "Will he remember it?"

"I don't know," I said. "I just started thinking, Braden knows about it too."

We did not go down the slope we had come up but went off through the trees, following Russell and not asking any questions.

I remember we crept down through a gully that was very thick with brush and near the bottom of it Russell held up. The open part was next and it was not dark enough to cross it.

When I think of all the waiting we did. It made being out there all the worse because it gave you time to imagine things. We kept quiet because Russell did. I have never seen a man so patient. He would sit with his legs crossed and fool with a stick or something, drawing with it in the sand, making circles and different signs and then smoothing out the sand and doing it all over again. What did a man like that think about? That's what I wondered about every time I looked at him.

From this gully you could not see anything but sky and the dark hump of the slope above us. I kept thinking that if I was back in Sweetmary I would have finished my supper and would be reading or going to visit somebody; seeing the main street then and the lanterns shining through the windows of the saloons; seeing lights way off in the adobes that were situated out from town.

There were some sounds around us, night sounds, which I took as a good sign; nothing was moving nearby. I heard the clicking sound of the McLaren girl's rosary beads, which I had not heard since the first evening in the stagecoach. It was funny, I had forgotten all about making conversation in order to get to know her. If I did not know her after this, I never would. It was something the way she never complained. But maybe she spoke out a little too quickly; even when she was right. That was something I never could do.

When the time came it was like always, coming after you had got tired of waiting for it and wondering when it ever would. There was Russell standing up again, like he knew or felt the exact moment we should leave, and within a few minutes we were down out of the gully with dark, wide-open country stretching out on three sides of us.

We did what Russell did. He didn't tell us. He kept in the lead and we followed with our eyes pretty much of the time. When he stopped, we stopped, which was often, though you could never guess when it was going to be. Or you could listen till your head ached and never know what made him stop.

All of us together made some noise moving through the brush clumps and kicking stones and things, which couldn't be helped. Just grit your teeth and hope nobody else heard it. Yet when Russell moved off from us to scout a little, which he did a few times, he never made a sound going or coming. His Apache-type moccasins had some-thing to do with it, but it was also the way he walked, a way I never learned.

You know how it is outside at night as far as seeing things, shapes and the sky and all. It is never as dark as indoors, in a cellar or in a closed room without a window. We would see a dark patch and it would turn out to be a brush thicket or some Joshua trees. There were those saguaros, but not as many as had been in the higher country. There was greasewood and prickly pear and other bushes I never knew the names of, most of them low to the ground so that you still felt yourself out in the open and unprotected.

I mentioned that Russell would stop and then we would, listening hard to make out some sound. We never heard anything except twice.

The first time, we were maybe halfway across, though it is hard to judge. I remember I was looking down at the ground, then up and I stopped all of a sudden seeing Russell standing still. He had turned and was facing us with his head raised a little.

Then we all heard it, thin and faraway but unmistakable, the sound of a gunshot.

We waited. A few minutes later it came again and seemed a little closer, though I could have imagined that. About ten seconds passed. A third gunshot sounded faintly, off in another direction, way off in the darkness.

Russell moved on, faster now, knowing they were still behind and not somewhere up ahead waiting. I was sure then that the gunshots were signals. Say they had split up to poke through that area where we had hid. Say one group found a sign of us (probably the Mexican) and signaled the others with a shot, then with another one when they did not answer at first. The third shot was when they did answer.

The McLaren girl thought differently. Right after the shots, as we went on, she said to me, "They've killed him."

I had forgotten about Dr. Favor until she said that. I explained what I thought about the signals.

"Maybe," she said. "But if they haven't killed him he'll die of thirst or starvation. He doesn't have any chance at all."

I said, "He sure didn't worry about us."

"Because he would do such a thing," the McLaren girl said, "should we?"

How do you answer a question like that? Anyway it wasn't us that did it, it was Russell. She certainly worried a lot without showing it on her face. I will say that for the McLaren girl.

The second time we heard a sound was a little later. This time it was a horse, sounding close, but far enough out so we couldn't see it. We went down flat and stayed that way for some time. We heard the horse again, never running or galloping, but walking, his shoes clinking against stones. It never came so close you could see it, but there was no doubting what it meant. They were out in the open now looking for us.

When Russell moved off finally it was at his careful, stopping, listening pace again. Nothing could hurry him, not even feeling them out here. He moved along with the Spencer down-pointed in one hand and the saddlebags over the other shoulder, like there wasn't anything in the world could make him hurry. Add that to what you know about his patience.

We saw the shape of the high ground ahead of us by the time we were halfway across. That's what made going slow so hard. There was cover staring right at you, but Russell chose to walk to it.

Finally he led us into some trees that was like going into a house and locking the door, and right away (which surprised nobody) we were climbing again. All the way up to the top of a ridge and along it instead of taking the pass that led into these hills. This part wasn't hard; it was even ground, grassy and with a lot of trees. But when we came to a higher ridge and Russell started climbing again, Mendez complained.

I don't think Russell even looked at him. He went on climbing and the rest of us followed: up through rocks and places you had to grab hold of roots and branches to pull yourself up. Then along a path that was probably a game trail, and finally on up to the top.

A couple of hundred yards along this ridge Russell stopped. There, down below us, was the San Pete mine works.

We had approached it the back way, from up above the shafts and crushing mill and all, which were on this side of the canyon. Way over on the other side you could make out the company buildings, even the one we had eaten breakfast in two days ago.

I think I would have bought John Russell a drink of liquor right then had there been any to buy. The McLaren girl and Mendez just stared; you could see the relief on their faces. That's what seeing something familiar did, letting you forget Braden for a minute and look ahead and start to see a little daylight.

At that point there was the sure feeling with all of us that we would make it to Delgado's without Braden ever getting close again. Except that just a little later on there was another familiar sight. One we had not counted on.

I am referring to Dr. Favor.

But I will get to that in a minute.

It was still dark as we came down the ridge toward the mine works. We didn't go down all the way, only about fifty or sixty feet to a level place where the open mine shafts and a shack were.

Farther along this shelf there was a shute built on scaffolding that went down to the big crushing mill located about forty or fifty yards down the grade. Ore tailings, which were slides of rock and sand and stuff that had been taken out of the shafts and dumped, formed long humps down on the other side of the crushing mill. Everything was quiet and there wasn't even a breeze moving.

As I have said, it was still dark, but you could make out the shapes of things down below: the crushing mill and ore tailings to the left of where we were; the company buildings about two hundred yards away, directly across the canyon from us.

We stood there for a few minutes, Russell looking over the works and I guess, thinking. Finally, when he spoke he said, "This is a good place." Meaning the shack up here on the shelf.

"There's more water for us down there," Mendez said, meaning the waterskin we'd left in that company building the day before yesterday.

Russell shook his head. "If we stay here all day, you want tracks leading up and down?"

"Stay!" Mendez said. The waiting was worrying his nerves. "Man, we're so close now!"

"If you go," Russell said, without any feeling at all, "you go back the way we came."

Mendez looked at him with those solemn eyes of his. He didn't say any more. We went inside the shack which was empty except for a couple of bats which we shooed out. On the two side walls were shelves that held bags of concentrate. (Evidently they had used this shack to test ore samples in.) We just stretched out on the dusty floor and used some of these bags as pillows.

Russell left the door part way open and laid

down his head near the opening. I laid down over by one of the windows. There were two of them in front, with board shutters you couldn't close.

Just one small thing: Russell did not offer his blanket to the McLaren girl, but used it himself. I offered mine to her again, as I had done the night before, and this time she took it. Figure that one out.

It was a few hours later, say between six and seven in the morning, after we had slept some and eaten and had our day's water, that we saw Dr. Favor again. The McLaren girl, by the right-hand window at the time, saw him first.

He was already down out of the south pass that approached the mine from the direction of that open country we had crossed. He was moving slow; dead tired you could see, his clothes messier and dirtier looking than before. He walked straight down the middle of the canyon in the sunlight and in the dead silence of those rickety buildings, looking up at the crushing mill for the longest time, then over at the line of company buildings.

Watching him, nobody said a word, waiting to see if he remembered the waterskin.

Alongside one of the buildings was a trough with a hand pump at one end of it. When Dr. Favor saw it, he ran over and started pumping. He fell on his knees and kept on pumping, his shoulders and arms moving up and down, up and down, keeping at it even when he must have known he wasn't going to get any water. After a few minutes he was pumping slower and slower. Finally he fell over the pump and held on there, not moving.

Inside the shack it was quiet as could be.

I remember when the McLaren girl spoke it was hardly above a whisper. I was by the other window with Mendez; Russell was by the door; but we all heard her. "He doesn't remember it," she said.

None of the others spoke.

"We have to tell him," she said then, calm and quiet about it, stating a fact, not just giving in to pity at the sight of him.

"We don't do anything," Russell said from the door. He kept his gaze on Dr. Favor who had sat down now, one arm still on the pump handle.

"You can look at that man," the McLaren girl said, "and not want to help him?" She was staring at Russell now.

"He'll move off," Russell said. "Then you won't have to look at him."

"But he's dying of thirst. You can *see* he is!"

"What did you think would happen?" Russell said. He looked at her then. "You didn't think you'd see him again. So yesterday was all right, uh?"

"If I didn't speak up yesterday," the McLaren girl said, "I was wrong."

"You'd feel better if he had run off with the water?"

"That has nothing to do with him down there now."

"But if you were down there," Russell said, "and he was up here."

"You just don't understand, do you?" the McLaren girl said.

Russell kept staring at her. "What do you want to do?"

"I want to help him!" She raised her voice a little, like she was running out of patience.

It didn't seem to bother Russell any. He said, "You want to go down to him? Make tracks on that slope that hasn't been touched in five years? You want to make signs pointing up where we are?"

"The man's dying of thirst!" She screamed it at Russell. She had run clean out of patience and threw the words right at him.

I don't mean she screamed so loud Dr. Favor heard her. He had now got up from the pump and was moving along the front of the company buildings, reaching the one we had stopped at the day before yesterday and looking up at it.

I held my breath again. Maybe he'd remembered the waterskin. But no, he went on by.

The next thing I knew the McLaren girl was out the window and running down the slope. Russell was out the door but too late to stop her. He stood there in front of the shack, Mendez and I by the window, and watched her raising little dust trails down the grade, seeing her getting smaller and smaller.

Near the bottom the McLaren girl called out. We saw Dr. Favor stop and look around. (He must have been surprised out of his shoes.) He started toward her, but she was yelling something at him now, motioning to the company building.

He stood there a second, then was almost running in his hurry to get to the building, the McLaren girl waiting now to see if he'd find the waterskin.

We were watching all this. We saw him reach the front of the place, just out from the shade formed by the veranda, and that's where he stopped. Right away he started backing off, like edging away. Next thing he had turned and was running toward the McLaren girl who didn't know what was going on anymore than we did and stood there watching him.

As he got close he must have said something. The McLaren girl started up the grade, looking back at the company building as she did.

About then was when he appeared. It was Early. He came out of the veranda shade, to the edge of it, and stood there with a Colt gun in one hand and a canteen in the other—evidently the canteen with whisky in it which the Mexican had mentioned to John Russell, for I think Early was drunk or close to it. The way he stood, his boots wide apart, looked like he was steadying himself. I won't swear to it because there wasn't time to get a good look at him.

He started firing his Colt, waving it toward us or at the McLaren girl and Dr. Favor as they came up the grade, causing Mendez and me to duck down, and firing until his gun was empty. He started yelling then, but we couldn't make out any of it.

I kept waiting for Braden and the others to appear, but they didn't. Not right then. Evidently Early had been sent on ahead, Braden figuring we would come this way.

I was still there at the window when the McLaren girl and Dr. Favor reached the shack. She came inside and went out again with the canteen and gave it to Dr. Favor who drank until she yanked it away from his mouth. He yanked back, held onto it and handed it to Russell. I think he could tell from looking at Russell that saving him had been just the McLaren girl's idea. He seemed to be smiling some, like the joke was on Russell.

"You will learn something about white people," he said to Russell. "They stick together."

"They better," Mendez said. "We all better."

Just for a second there was the old tell-nothing

Henry Mendez talking. It sounded good after seeing the other side of him for two days. He wasn't looking at Dr. Favor. I noticed then Russell was looking off down the slope too.

Like they had been following Dr. Favor (and no doubt they had), there came the Mexican on foot, Frank Braden and the Favor woman each on a horse, this little procession coming down out of the south pass, keeping close to the other side and in no hurry at all. The Mexican raised his arm up and waved.

We were all back together again. Right back where we had started. Except now we were up on that shelf of rock, looking down and seeing them moving up canyon and dismounting in front of the company building that was straight across from us and drawing their rifles.

You think about an awful lot of things at once. That we should be doing something; getting out of there or doing *something*. That this never should have happened. That if it wasn't for the McLaren girl and her act of kindness to a man who didn't deserve it, they never would have found us; they would have looked up at that bare unmarked slope and gone right on. Maybe you would like to have said something to the McLaren girl. It was a temptation. But only Mendez did.

He said, "You see?" looking at Dr. Favor and then at the McLaren girl in the doorway. "You see?" he said again, wanting to say more, but just shaking his head as he thought of everything at once.

The McLaren girl had been quiet, but I think Mendez made her mad. She said, "I'd do it again. Knowing they were there I'd do it again. What do you think of that!"

"He's not worth it!" Mendez said, keeping his teeth together so he wouldn't scream it at her. Still it was loud.

"Who are you to say who's worth it!" When she got mad, she spoke out, as you have seen.

Dr. Favor didn't get into it. He was running his tongue over his swollen lips, I think still tasting the water.

And Russell. Russell, still outside squatted down, sitting back on his heels. He was smoking a cigarette, gazing over across the canyon. Russell didn't look at the McLaren girl (not then) or say anything to anybody. Russell was Russell.

He just smoked the cigarette as he watched Braden and the others over in front of the company building, watching them take the two horses into the shade of the built-up, second-story veranda, watching the Mexican come out again in the sunlight and walk up and down in a show-offy way, his hands on his hips and looking up toward where we were.

That's when Russell came inside the shack. Next thing I knew he was at the other window with the Spencer at his shoulder. I doubt the Mexican saw him. I'm sure he didn't else he would have done something before Russell fired.

With the sound of the shot and dust kicking up in front of him, the Mexican stopped dead. Russell fired again and this time the Mexican jumped back into the veranda shade. Russell was not taking anything off that Mexican.

"What do you start that for?" Mendez said, sounding pained.

Russell must have thought there was an awful lot of dumb questions asked. He said to Mendez, "So they'd see us."

Nobody down there returned the fire, but we kept expecting it. Everybody was inside by then. Russell was already piling those bags of concentrate on his window sill. I started building up the other one then, the McLaren girl helping. Mendez brought a few over to Russell, but Dr. Favor didn't lift a hand. He was doing his thinking now, I guess, and eying the saddlebags. Since Russell didn't say anything to him, I didn't either. Hell.

Next Russell pulled the loading tube out of his Spencer and stuck two more cartridges in it from his belt. I kept by the other window wondering if this little revolver I had would do any good.

The minutes went by but the awful nervous feeling I had and tried not to show didn't ease up any.
I remember wondering if Russell was scared. He
had taken his hat off and I could see the side of his
face good. As I have said before, he looked so
much younger with his hat off and his hair pressed
down on his forehead. He would swallow or
scratch his nose, things everybody did, and he
didn't seem any different than the rest of us.

Only he was different. As Braden was about to
learn first hand.

Frank Braden's idea was to let us worry some, I
suppose. About a half hour passed before we heard
from him. Then it came all of a sudden.

He yelled out from across the way, "You hear
me!" He waited. "I'm coming up to talk! You hold
your fire!" He waited and yelled again. Maybe a
minute passed.

Then Braden appeared at the edge of the veranda shade. Early and the Mexican were behind
him. They waited there as Braden moved out from
them carrying a Winchester rifle and a white cloth
or something tied to the end of it. Frank Braden's
idea of a truce flag.

Russell watched him. As Braden came across the
open, out in the sunlight and without any cover
close by, Russell raised the Spencer and eared back
the hammer.

"He wants to talk," Mendez said. "You heard him. It's no trick. He's got something to say to us!"

Russell didn't bother with Mendez or even look up. He steadied the Spencer on the ore-sample bags and put the front sight on Braden.

5

Frank Braden had nerve. You can put that under his name big. A man does not hold up stage-coaches without nerve, or walk up an open grade in plain sight of people he knows are armed.

If he was afraid at all, he never showed it. The way his hat was funneled and tipped forward over his eyes he had to raise his head to look up. He kept watching, but it did not make him hesitate. He came across the open from the company building like nothing in the world bothered him, the Winchester raised a little and the white truce flag tied to the end of it.

He was putting his faith in that truce flag and the fact that the Mexican had done the same thing yesterday without drawing fire. It showed he still didn't know John Russell very well.

Russell was letting him come. He never took the Spencer away from his shoulder, but the barrel kept lowering a hair at a time as Braden came closer. Anyone else might have been covering Braden; but somehow you knew Russell meant to fire on him, else he never would have raised the gun. The question was how close Braden would get.

"Listen—he just wants to talk," Mendez said, moving toward Russell as you would approach a bronc with your hand out to gentle it. "You can see it's no trick. The man is coming to *talk*. Can't you see that? You want to start something when there's no need to?

"Look at me!"

Russell's head raised up a little, interrupted from what he was concentrating on. But he kept his eyes on Braden who had now reached some ore-cart tracks that came across from the crushing mill and past a little shack on out into the open a ways. On this side of the tracks Braden was less than a hundred yards off. He kept coming.

"Just see what he wants," Mendez said. "You don't have to talk to him. You don't want to, one of us will." Mendez looked outside, seeing Braden on the grade now and starting up.

"You don't know what he wants. Man, you got to find out what he wants," Mendez kept saying. "Listen to him. He trusts us . . . we have to trust him and see what he wants. Doesn't that make sense to you?" Mendez said it all fast. If it didn't convince Russell, it bothered him enough so he couldn't concentrate on Braden.

By that time Braden was part way up the grade.

He stopped there and yelled out, "Anybody home?"

Mendez saw the opportunity looking at him and he grabbed a hold of it. "We hear you!" he yelled back.

"Come on out of that boar's nest," Braden called. "We'll talk some."

"Say what you want," Mendez answered.

"I thought maybe you'd like to go home."

"Say something," Mendez said.

"It's looking at you," Braden said back. "We can sit here long as we want. I can send a man for more water and chuck, but you people can't move. You only move if we let you. You see that?"

"What else?"

"There doesn't have to be much else."

"All right, what do you want?"

"You leave the money, we leave the woman."

"And everybody goes home?"

"Everybody goes home."

"We'll have to talk about it."

"You do that." Braden held the Winchester cradled over one arm, the truce flag hanging limp. He stood with his feet spread some, posing, it looked like, confident he knew what he was doing.

"We'll let you look at the woman while you talk," Braden said. "Then when you're ready you bring the money down and take the woman."

"We'll talk about it," Mendez said again. He

glanced over at Dr. Favor who was at the other window, then down at Braden again.

"What if," he said "—well, what if nobody wants this woman?"

"Wait a while," Braden answered, "before you think anything like that."

"I just want to make sure what you mean, that's all."

"You just have to be sure of one thing," Braden said. "You don't leave here with the money. You see that?"

Mendez didn't answer. Frank Braden waited a minute then started to go.

"Hey," Russell called out to him and Braden stopped, half way around so that he was looking back over his shoulder.

"I got a question," Russell said.

Braden was squinting to make out Russell in the window. "Ask it," he said.

"How you going to get down that hill?"

Braden knew what he meant. He stood there a moment, then came around slowly to face the shack again, showing us he wasn't afraid.

"Look, I come up here to tell you how things are. I'm making it easy on you."

"We didn't ask you," Russell said. "You walk up here yourself. You come and say we're not leaving with the money . . . uh?"

"You heard what I said." Braden was tenser, you could tell.

"We give you the money or you kill us."

"I said you wouldn't leave here."

"But it's the same thing, uh? . . . Maybe we give up the money and you still kill us."

"You better talk to your friends."

"I think," Russell kept on, "you want to leave dead people who can't tell things."

"If that was so, we'd have killed you at the stagecoach."

"You tried to," Russell said, "taking the water. But it came back to us."

"You think what you want," Braden said, meaning to end it.

Russell nodded. He nodded up and down very slowly two or three times. "I've already thought," he said in that mild way, so calm you did not suspect what he meant until he raised the Spencer. Then there was no doubt what he meant.

"You hold on, boy!" Braden said. "I'm walking down the same way I come up." But he was backing off, keeping his gaze fixed on the window.

Russell had the Spencer at his shoulder, but his head up as he watched Braden.

"You hear me!" Braden yelled. "You hold on!"

It was like Russell was letting out rope, giving Braden a little slack before he yanked it tight. It was coming. We knew it and Braden, still backing away, knew it. But only Russell knew when. That's what finally spooked Braden. He might have had seven miles of nerve inside of him, but all of a sudden he found it all let out and there was only one thing left to do.

He started running, starting so fast across the slope toward the crushing mill that he fell within four or five steps, falling just as Russell pressed his face to that Spencer and fired. Maybe that fall saved Braden's life; for certain it hurried Russell's second shot, trying to get Braden while he was down, but that one kicked sand right in front of Braden who was lunging to his feet, running again, getting some distance as Russell took his time and aimed and when he fired again Braden twisted and rolled a ways down the slope. That's when the gunfire opened up from the company building as the Mexican and Early woke up and started giving Braden some cover. Braden was crawling, then up on his feet and running again, limping-running, favoring one leg—and *bam*, the Spencer went off and Braden was knocked down again, down on his hands and knees, but somehow kept going, clawing the ground and half running half crawling, the Winchester truce flag behind him now and forgotten. Russell fired again, hurrying it because Braden was close to the crushing mill by then and that was Russell's last one; Braden made it, reaching the corner of the building, about forty yards over from us, as the sound of Russell's shot sang off down canyon.

It was the Mexican who got Braden out of there. He came up over on the other side of the crushing mill and brought Braden down the same way, keeping the crushing mill between us and them so they wouldn't get shot at.

Early came out of the veranda shade to help the Mexican take Braden inside: Early looking back like he was afraid Russell would open up again, and Braden walking but dragging his legs and leaning on the two men. He had been shot up good.

Mr. Braden, I thought to myself. Meet John Russell.

But was our situation any better?

Maybe. Depending on Braden. If he was hurt bad enough, they would have to get him to a bed or a doctor. So for a while we watched with that hope. But the hope kept getting smaller and smaller as time passed and nobody rode out from the company building.

When there was no doubt but they were staying, Henry Mendez started on Russell again. Why did you have to do that? Why didn't you let things just happen? he kept saying. It would be worse for us now, Mendez was sure. And it was Russell's fault.

"Nothing is different," Russell said. In other words, they could be mad or shot up or hungry or drunk, they'd still try to kill us. When you thought about it, you knew it was true.

While Mendez and Russell were together I brought up the idea of getting out the way we'd come in.

They'd shoot us off the wall as we climbed up, was Mendez's answer. "Not when it's dark," Russell said; you saw he was thinking of ways.

So far, you will notice, no one had said Russell should give them the money in exchange for Mrs. Favor: do what Braden wanted and *see* what would happen, not just guess. Maybe because it would be wasting breath to mention it to Russell. Or maybe because no one was thinking of Mrs. Favor at that time.

Well, that changed as soon as the Mexican brought her out. Maybe an hour had passed from the time Braden was shot. (It's hard to remember now the different spaces of time.) It had been so quiet over there. Then the Mexican was coming out across the open with Mrs. Favor in front of him. Her hands were tied and there was a length of rope, like a dog leash, tied around her neck with the Mexican holding the other end.

He brought her all the way out to the ore-cart tracks that came down from the crushing mill and made her sit down there. Kneeling, he tied the leash to one of the rails, keeping Mrs. Favor in front of him as he did. He drew his left-hand Colt then, holding his right elbow tight against his side, and ran to a little shed that was just above and over a few yards.

He surprised us then. Instead of going back, keeping the shed in line with us as a cover, he made a run all the way across a pretty open stretch to the crushing mill.

Picture him about forty yards down and over to our left; Mrs. Favor straight down, looking small sitting there and staring up at the shack, about eighty yards away.

It was while the Mexican was making his run that Early came out carrying a rifle and moved off toward the south pass on foot. I did not have to think about it long. Early was circling around to get behind us, closing the back door whether we wanted to use it or not.

That's what Russell said too. He was still at the window watching the corner of the crushing mill where the Mexican was. The McLaren girl asked him where Early was going and Russell said, "Behind us," not taking his eyes off the crushing mill; the Mexican had not shown himself yet.

Dr. Favor, at this time, was at the other window looking down at his wife. It was a strange thing, while he was there no one else went out to the window, as if letting him be alone with her. But he did not stay too long; he walked away and lit up a cigar and sat down, I guess to think some more.

The McLaren girl and Mendez and I finally found ourselves at that window, where we stayed just about all the rest of the time we were there. Of course we kept looking at Mrs. Favor.

Remember Braden saying, "We'll let you look at the woman while you talk?" He knew what he was doing.

She sat there between the ore-cart tracks looking up this way most of the time. We soon learned that she could not stand up straight; the rope tied to her neck was not long enough. She could get in a bent-over position, but that was all. For a time she tried to undo the rope end tied to the track, but evidently the Mexican had tied it too tight.

So she just sat there out in the open with the sun getting higher all the time, sometimes brushing her hair out of her face or picking things off her skirt. The way she would look up— my gosh—you knew what she was thinking. But she certainly was calm about it, not even crying once. It was not till a little later we found out they had not given her any water.

It was after the Mexican started on Russell.

He yelled out from the corner of the crushing mill, just showing part of his head for a second, "Hey, *hombre!* How do you like that woman? . . .

You want her? . . . We give her to you!" Things like that.

John Russell did not answer. Except he put his face against the stock of the Spencer and the front sight on the corner of the crushing mill.

The Mexican waited a while. Then he yelled, "If you want that, *hombre*, you better hurry! Maybe there won't be nothing left in the sun!"

It was about 10 o'clock by then, maybe a little earlier.

Then the Mexican yelled, "Man, why don't you come out and give her a drink of water? She hasn't had none . . . not since yesterday morning!"

There he was, just a little part of him at the corner, and *bam* the Spencer went off and you saw the wood splinter right where the Mexican's face had been.

It was quiet right after, long enough for us to wonder if Russell had got him. Long enough for the McLaren girl to say, "That woman hasn't had any water." Then to Russell: "Did you hear what he said? She hasn't had water since yesterday."

Russell was watching the corner still. The McLaren girl kept staring at him. "Is that why you want to kill him?" she said then. "To shut him up? So you won't have to hear about her?"

I touched her arm to calm her, but she jerked away. "It won't help to get fighting among ourselves," I said.

"Are we all on the same side?" she said. "Do you really think that?"

"Well, we're all sitting here."

She was looking at Russell again. "He's sitting here with twelve thousand dollars of somebody else's money and that woman is tied like an animal out there in the sun." She looked at me like somebody should do something.

"Well, what do you want him to do?"

The McLaren girl never answered. The Mexican yelled out again, letting us know he was still alive. "Hey, *hombre*!" he called out. "You got wood in my eyes! . . . Come down here and help me get it out!" Honest to gosh, like he thought it was funny to be shot at.

He kept it up, yelling at Russell from time to time, trying to get him outside. We heard from Early a few times too. Rocks coming down on the roof from above: Early still feeling his whisky and being playful, or else just letting us know he was up there and not to try anything.

The McLaren girl was quiet for a while. I guess she had calmed down. The sole of one of her shoes was loose and she kept fooling with it, trying to twist it off, even when she was looking at Mrs. Favor who sat with her shoulders hunched over now and her head down. The McLaren girl could not look at her too long, or fool with that shoe forever.

She started looking at Russell and finally went over and kneeled down next to him. Russell was smoking, sitting back on his feet, the Spencer resting on the ore bags lining the window sill.

"We have to give them the money," she said, very quietly, "I think you know that."

He looked at her, not just glancing but taking his time to look at her dark sun-browned face good.

"Like you had to give that one water," Russell said. Meaning Dr. Favor.

"That's over with." She bristled up a little.

"You think he would have done it for you?"

"Somebody would have."

"How do you know that?"

"I just know. People help other people."

"People kill other people too."

"I've seen that."

"You're going to see some more."

"If you want to say it's my fault we're stuck here, go ahead," the McLaren girl said. "It might make you feel better, but it won't change anything."

Russell shook his head. "The thing I want to know is why you helped."

"Because he *needed* help! I didn't ask if he deserved it!"

She let her temper calm down and said, half as

loud, "Like that woman needs to live. It's not up to us to decide if she deserves it."

"We only help her, uh?"

"Do we have another choice?"

Russell nodded. "Not help her."

"Just let her die." The McLaren girl kept staring at him.

"That's up to Braden," Russell said. "We have another thing to look at. If we don't give him the money, he has to come get it."

The McLaren girl almost let go of her temper then. "You'd sacrifice a human life for that money. That's what you're saying."

Russell started making a cigarette, looking out the window at the crushing mill as he shaped it, then at the McLaren girl again. "Go ask that woman what she thinks of human life. Ask her what a human life is worth at San Carlos when they run out of meat."

"That isn't any fault of hers."

"She said those dirty Indians eat dogs. You remember that? She couldn't eat a dog no matter how hungry she was." Everybody was watching him. He lit his cigarette and blew out smoke. "Go ask her if she'd eat a dog now."

"That's why!" the McLaren girl said, like it was all clear to her now. "She insulted the poor hungry miserable Indians and you'd let her die for that!"

Russell shook his head. "We were talking about human life."

"Even if there was no money, nothing to be gained, you'd let her die!" All the McLaren girl's temper was showing now, and she was just letting it come. "Because she thinks Indians are dirty and no better than animals you'd sit there and let her die!"

Russell held the cigarette close to his mouth, watching her. "It makes you angry, why talk about it?"

"I want to talk about it," she shot back. "I would like you to ask me what I think a human life is worth . . . a dirty human Apache life. Go on, ask me. Ask me about the ones that took me from my home and kept me past a month. Ask me about the dirty things they did, what the women did when the men weren't around and what the men did when we weren't running but were hiding somewhere and there was time to waste. I dare you to ask me!"

She knelt there tensed, like she was to spring on him if he moved, though it was just she was so intent on telling him what she'd just said.

It was all out of her system then. I think everybody wasn't so tense anymore. She sank back to a sitting position, taking her eyes off Russell, looking down at that loose sole on her shoe and fooling with it as she thought something over.

Next thing, she was saying, "I haven't seen my folks in almost two months ... or my little brother. Just he and I were home and he ran and I don't know what happened to him, whether they caught him or what."

She looked up at Russell again, all the softness gone out of her that quick, like it was starting all over again. "What do they think of an eight-year-old human life?" she said. "Do they just kill little boys who can't defend themselves?"

Russell had not taken his eyes off her, still holding the cigarette up near his face. "If they don't want them," he said, and kept looking right at her.

That ended it. For a thin little seventeen-year-old girl she was tougher than most men and I think you know that by now. But she had to give some time. I thought she was going to cut at Russell again, but the words didn't come. Her eyes filled up first. She sat there trying to keep her chin from quivering or crying so we'd hear her, still looking right at Russell even with her eyes wet, daring him to say something else.

Right at that time (and it was almost welcome) the Mexican started again. He yelled out, "Hey man, you hear me!" Russell turned and looked down the barrel of the Spencer. The Mexican wasn't showing himself now and his voice sounded a little farther away. You knew he was there though.

"Come on down here," the Mexican yelled out, "I got something for you!"

Russell had something for him too if he showed even part of his face.

"Man!" the Mexican yelled then. "We both come out—talk to each other!"

He waited.

"You bring that piece of iron you got. I bring one, uh?"

Every word he yelled echoed up canyon and came back again.

"Hey, *hombre*, whatever your name is—you hear me!"

After that he said some things I had better not put down here, terrible words that were embarrassing to hear with the McLaren girl in the same room. He was trying to get Russell out by insulting him, but he could have been yelling at a tree stump for all the good it did. Russell sat there waiting for the Mexican to show himself; which he never did.

Something Russell had said to the McLaren girl bothered me, so I asked him about it: about them having to come up here if they wanted the money. Why couldn't they just outwait us? Our water would run out (there was about a quart and a half left), then what would we do?

Theirs would run out too, Russell said. But, I said, they can go get more.

All the way to Delgado's? Russell said. Who

would go, the one up behind us? The Mexican? Then who would watch us? No, Russell said. Some time they have to come up here. They know it.

I said that may be, but the Favor woman would be dead by then. Russell didn't answer.

About two o'clock in the afternoon the Favor woman started screaming.

It could not get any hotter than it was then. There was no breeze, no clouds; the sun was bright, boiling hot and you would not even dare look up to see where it was.

The Favor woman sat down there near the bottom of the grade, no hat or anything to cover her head, no shade to crawl into. As I have said, there was a little shack near where she was, but the rope tied to her neck would not even let her stand up straight much less get over to the shack. She had given up trying to undo the rope.

For the longest time she sat hunched over, her face buried in her arm resting on her raised knees. Now she was looking up toward us, as she had done when the Mexican first put her there, and now every once in a while she would scream out to her husband, calling his name at first.

"Alex!" she would call, but drawn out and faint sounding, not sharp and loud as you would imagine a real scream.

"Alex . . . help me!" Sounding far away almost,

like hearing only an echo of the words. She had not had water since yesterday. It was something that she could call out at all.

Dr. Favor raised up when she started and looked down at her for a while. I don't know what he was thinking. I don't even know if he felt sorry for her, because his expression never changed; he was just looking at something. He didn't call back to her or say a word.

Some people can hide their feelings very well, so I had better not pass judgment on Dr. Favor. I remember picturing him and his wife alone and wondering what they ever talked about and if they had ever got along well together. (I couldn't help having that feeling she had been just a woman to him. You know what I mean, just a woman to have around.) I tried to imagine her calling him Alex when they were alone. But it didn't sound right. He was not the kind of man you thought of as having a first name. Especially not a name like Alex or Alexander.

There it was though, faintly, coming from out of that big open canyon, "Alex . . ." And he just sat there looking down at her, not moving much other than to feel his beard, to rub it gently under his chin with the back of his fingers.

Once she stood up, as far as she could, and yelled his name louder than she ever did before. "Alex!" And this time it was sharp and clear enough and with an echo coming back to give you goose pimples at the sound of it.

And then again, which I will hear every day of my life.

"Alex . . . please help me!" The words all alone outside, echoing and fading to nothing.

It was strange to be in a room with four people and not hear one sound. Everybody sat there holding still, waiting for the Favor woman to cry out again. Maybe a couple of minutes passed; maybe more than that, it seemed longer. It was so quiet that when the sound came—the sound of a match scraping and popping aflame—everybody looked up and right at John Russell.

He lit his cigarette, shook the match out and threw it up past his shoulder, out the window.

The McLaren girl, closer to the window where Mendez and I still were, kept staring at Russell. Do you see how his calm rubbed her? I think any of the rest of us could have lit a cigarette at that time and it would have been all right. But not Russell. Lighting that match touched it off again. Just the way she was looking at him you could see it coming, so I tried to head it off.

I said, "I've been thinking"—though I hadn't, it just came to me then—"when it gets dark, why can't a couple of us sneak down and get her? Maybe we could get her up here without them even seeing us."

"But if they heard you—" Mendez said.

"By dark she'll be dead," the McLaren girl said.

"You don't *know* that," I said.

"Do you want to wait and find out?"

"I was thinking something else," I said. "Braden's watching her too. What if he sees it's not working or he feels sorry for her or something and has that Mexican bring her back in?"

"You just think nice things, don't you?" the McLaren girl said.

"It could happen."

"The day he changes into a human being." She looked at Russell smoking his cigarette. "Or the day *he* does. That's the only thing will save her."

Russell was watching her, but just then the Mexican yelled out from the crushing mill, and Russell's head turned to look down the barrel of the Spencer.

"Hey, *hombre*!" the Mexican yelled, followed by a string of words some of which were in Spanish and were probably as obscene as the English ones mixed in. "Come on down and see me!"

Russell kept looking down the Spencer for at least a minute. When he turned to us again, he drew on his cigarette and dropped it out the window. The hand came down on the saddlebags next to him. He lifted them up, feeling the weight of them, then let them swing a little and threw them so they fell out in the middle of the floor.

"You want to save her?" Russell said. He

looked at Mendez and me and then over to Dr. Favor sitting with his back to the wall a few feet from me. "Somebody want to walk down there and save her?"

Nobody answered.

"Somebody wants to, go ahead," Russell said. "But I'll tell you one thing first. You walk down there you won't walk back. Leave that bag and start to take the woman and they'll kill both of you."

The McLaren girl was watching him, leaning forward a little. "You're saying that so nobody will take the money and try it."

"They'll kill both of you," Russell said. "That's why I'm saying it." He looked over at Dr. Favor before the McLaren girl could say anything else.

"That woman's your wife," Russell said to him. "You want to go untie her?"

Dr. Favor, his head down a little, had his eyes on Russell, but he didn't say one word.

Russell took his time, making it awful embarrassing, so you wouldn't dare look over at Dr. Favor. Finally Russell turned to us again.

"Mr. Mendez," he said, "you want to save her? . . . Or Mr. Carl Allen, I think your name is, you want to walk down there? This man won't. It's his wife, but he won't do it. He doesn't care about his own woman, but maybe someone else does, uh? That's what I want to know."

He was looking right at the McLaren girl then and said, "I don't think I know your name. We live together some, uh? But I don't know your name."

"Kathleen McLaren," she said. He must have surprised her, caught her without anything else ready to say.

"All right, Kathleen McLaren," Russell said. "How would you like to walk down there and untie her and start up again and get shot in the back? Or in the front if that one by the mill does it. In the back or in the front, but one way or the other."

She kept looking at him but didn't say a word.

"There it is," Russell said, nodding to the saddlebags. "Take it. You worry more about his wife than he does. You say I'm not sure or I'm not telling the truth—all right, you go find out what happens."

Russell did a strange thing then. He took off his Apache moccasins and threw them over to the McLaren girl.

"Wear those," he said. "You run faster when they start shooting."

He opened up his blanket and took out his boots and pulled them on. While he did, the McLaren girl kept staring at him; but she never spoke. And when he looked up at her again, her eyes held only for a second before looking away.

It was one thing to know a woman would die if

she didn't get help. It was another thing to say you'd die helping her.

I kept thinking of what Russell had said right to me ". . . do you want to walk down there?"

No, I didn't, and I will admit that right here. I believed Braden would shoot anybody who went down there with the money. I think everybody believed it by then. Yes, even the McLaren girl.

The best thing to do, I decided, was just sit there and wait and see what happened. That sounds like a terrible thing to say when a woman's life is at stake, Mrs. Favor's; but I will tell you now it's easier to think of your own life than someone else's. I don't care how brave a person is.

I will admit, too, that Dr. Favor being there made it easier on your conscience. If anybody should go down there it was him. He wasn't going though; that was certain.

Some more time passed. The Mexican, who was patient and had as much time as we did, yelled out at Russell once in a while. Russell stayed with his face pressed to that Spencer longer every time the Mexican insulted him or tried to draw him out. You could see Russell was anxious to get the Mexican. After quite a while passed and the Mexican did not yell at him again, Russell turned around to lean against the wall and make a cigarette. I noticed he threw the tobacco sack away after. It was his last one. He did not light it though; not yet.

Time passed as we sat there and nobody said a word. Russell was thinking, working something out and picturing how it would be; I was sure of that.

About four o'clock the Favor woman started screaming for her husband again; the sounds coming not so loud as before, but it was an awful thing to hear. She would call his name, then say something else which was never clear but like she was pleading with him to help her.

Sitting there in the shack you heard it faintly out in the canyon, "Alex"—the name drawn out, then again maybe and the rest of the words coming like a long moan.

It was quiet when Russell stood up. He looked out the window, not long, just a minute or so, then went over and picked up the grainsack, emptying out what meat and bread and coffee were left, and brought it back to the window. He took one of the ore bags from the sill and put it in the sack. Nobody else moved, all of us watching him. That was when he lit his last cigarette. He drew on it very slowly, very carefully. We kept watching him, maybe not trusting him either, knowing he was about to do something.

"I need somebody," Russell said, looking right at me. Not knowing what he meant I just sat there. "Right here," he said, nodding to the window.

I went over, not in any hurry, staring at him to

show I didn't understand. But he didn't explain until he'd motioned again and I was kneeling there with the stock of his Spencer between us. Russell put his hand on it.

"You know how to shoot this?"

"I'm not sure." Frowning at him.

"Push the trigger guard down with your thumb. That ejects and loads . . . uh? Right now it's ready and maybe you only need the one." He added, almost under his breath, "Man, I hope you only need one."

I said, "I'm going to shoot at them?"

"The one by the mill." Russell looked out the window. "He'll come across and walk past that shack by the woman and stand with his back to you, up this way from the shack a little. Then, be sure then, you keep the front sight on him."

"I don't understand what you mean," I said.

"What's there to understand?" There was just a little surprise in his voice, mostly it was quiet and patient. "If he touches his gun, you shoot him."

"But," I said, "in the *back*?"

"I'll ask him if he'll turn around," Russell said.

"Look," I said, "I just don't understand what's going to happen. That's what I'm talking about."

"You'll see it," Russell said. He thought a minute. "Maybe you have to see something else. The money—that it gets up to San Carlos."

"Look, if you'd just explain—"

He touched my arm. "Maybe it's you who has to take it up to San Carlos after. That's easy, uh?"

I kept staring at him. "You never were keeping it for yourself, were you?"

He just looked at me—like he was tired—or like what was the use explaining now?

He put his hat on, straight and pulled down a little over his eyes. He picked up the grainsack, swinging it up over his left shoulder. All of us were watching him, the McLaren girl never moving.

She kept staring and said, "You're going." Just those two words.

Russell made a little shrugging motion. "Maybe try something."

"What if they don't think you've got the money in there?"

"They come out and see," Russell answered.

"They might," the McLaren girl nodded. "They just might."

"They have to," Russell said.

The McLaren girl kept staring at him, wanting to ask why he was doing it, I think. But Russell was looking at Mendez then. "You'll watch this Dr. Favor. Good this time?" he said.

Mendez said something in Spanish and Russell answered also in Spanish, shrugging his shoulders. Mendez appeared like he was afraid to breathe. Russell turned to Dr. Favor. He had something for everybody.

"All that trouble you went to, uh?"

Dr. Favor didn't answer, not caring what anybody said or thought about him now. He sat there staring up at Russell, his big face pale-looking with that reddish hair around it and with hardly any expression. He probably thought this John Russell was the biggest fool God ever made.

We were watching him, every one of us; perhaps still not certain he was going down there and having to see it to believe it.

He was at the door when the McLaren girl picked up his moccasins and threw them over to him. "Wear those," she said. "You run faster when they start shooting."

Do you see what she was doing? Giving it right back to him. Using the same words even that he had used before. Saying it calmly and watching to see his reaction.

And seeing his smile then; a smile you were sure he meant. Even with his hat on, at that moment he looked young and like anybody else.

Russell stood with his hand on the door, looking over his shoulder at the McLaren girl, at her only.

"Maybe we should talk more sometime," he said.

"Maybe," the McLaren girl answered. She was looking at him the same way, intently, like seeing something in him that was not there before. "When things calm down," she said.

I had the feeling she wanted to say more than that, but she didn't.

Russell nodded, his strange light-blue-colored eyes not moving from the girl's. "When things calm down," he said back.

He pulled the door open and stepped outside with the grainsack over his shoulder. The next time I was close enough to John Russell to see his face, he was dead.

Not long ago I was talking to a man from Benson who said they were playing a song now about Frank Braden and the woman he stole for reasons of love, and that I would appreciate it. I said are they playing a song about John Russell? He said who is John Russell?

What took place that afternoon at the San Pete mine has been written many times and different ways. (Including the song now.) Maybe you have read some of them. All I want to say is the account that appeared in the *Florence Enterprise* is a true one, even to the number of shots that were fired. Except even that account does not tell enough. (Which is what caused me to write this.) It describes a man named John Russell; but you still do not know John Russell after you have read it.

I am not saying anything against the *Florence Enterprise*. Their account was written in one hour or so, just telling what happened. I have been writing this for three months trying to tell you about John Russell as he was, so you will understand him. Yet, after three months of writing and thinking and all, I can't truthfully say I understand him myself. I only feel I know why he walked down that slope.

I watched him from the window. I was also keeping an eye out for the Mexican. The Mexican must have seen Russell as he started down, but he did not come out from the crushing mill until Russell was about half way.

That was when Russell held up the grainsack. "Hey!" He yelled out, the same way the Mexican had been yelling at him, "I got something for you!"

The Mexican was being careful as he moved across the grade, keeping his eyes on Russell all the time. By then the Favor woman had seen him; sitting stooped over, her hair hanging and straggly, she was watching him come.

Russell did not look at the Mexican, though he must have known the Mexican was moving down and across the grade as if to head him off. By then you could see part of the Mexican's back. I got down lower and, as Russell had instructed, put the front sight of the Spencer square on him, getting an awful feeling as I did.

At that moment, Early, up above us on the ridge, was probably putting his sights on Russell.

I kept expecting the Mexican to do something; but as he got over more by that little shack he slowed up so that he was hardly moving; not taking his eyes from Russell for a second, his right elbow bent and the elbow pressed against where he had been shot, his left hand hanging free. That was the hand I had watched, feeling the trigger of the Spencer and ready to pull it if the hand went to the Colt gun alongside it.

The Mexican stopped.

He was almost in line but a little to the left; so that from here you would look down past his right side to Russell who was nearing the Favor woman. She did not call out or appear to have said a word; she just kept staring at him, maybe not believing what she saw.

It was as Russell reached her that Frank Braden showed himself.

Braden came out of the veranda shade. He was limping some, I think trying not to show it, though he kept his left hand on his thigh, gripping it with his fingers spread.

The Mexican had not moved. I kept sighting on him, trying to watch Braden and Russell at the same time. Russell was kneeling by the woman, not paying any attention to Braden who kept coming. Braden called something, but Russell did not look up.

Braden called out again, slowing up and ready, you could tell.

Russell rose to his feet, helping the Favor woman as he did and you saw she was untied now. You also saw the grainsack lying over on the other side of the ore-cart tracks.

Russell and the Favor woman had taken only a few steps when Braden called out again. This time Russell stopped, though he motioned the Favor woman to keep going. She did, but looking back as Russell stood there watching Braden. She got up as high as the Mexican. He paid no attention to her. She was walking kind of sideways, coming up but looking back all the time.

The next thing I knew the front of the Spencer was on her. She had wandered just enough, looking back and not watching where she was going, to get behind the Mexican. I looked up, about to yell at her, but didn't. The Mexican would hear it too.

All I could do was keep telling her to get out of the way in my mind. Please hurry up and get out of the way.

Braden had reached the grainsack. He stood by it saying something to Russell who was about ten feet from him. Russell answered him. (What this was about, no one knows. Braden could have said to open the sack, show him the money. Russell would have told him to look in it himself if he doubted it was there.)

The Favor woman looked up at where we were. I stood up and waved my arm, but as I did she was looking back the other way again.

Even standing and sighting down with the Spencer against the side frame, the Favor woman was still in the way. I could only see part of the Mexican.

In my mind I kept telling her over and over again to get out of the way, to please, for the Lord's sake move one way or the other and to *hurry*! Now, right now, just move or look up here again or sit down or do *something*!

She stood there. She turned around to watch what was happening below and did not move from the spot.

Braden, his left hand still holding his thigh, straightened the grainsack with his boot toe so that the open end was toward him. Russell watched.

Braden went down to one knee, his right one, and now the hand came away from his thigh and unloosened the opening of the grainsack. Russell watched.

Braden straightened up, still kneeling. He said something to Russell. What? Warning him? Telling him not to try anything because the Mexican was behind him?

I saw Braden's hand reach inside the grainsack. Move! I thought. Get somewhere else!

If there was time—

Just move! I actually heard it in my mind, and I was to the door and out the door, running along the shelf, seven, eight, ten yards to be sure of the angle, to be sure of not hitting the woman.

But I had not even brought up the gun to aim when Braden's hand came out of the grainsack. He was rising, trying to get out his revolver, but was already too late. Russell drew and fired twice with his Colt extended and aimed . . . his other arm coming up as he fired the second round and he was stumbling forward as if kicked in the back. The Mexican had pulled his long-barreled .44 and fired three shots in the time Russell had hit Braden twice and Braden and Russell both went down, Russell to his hands and knees, but turning with his revolver already raised and he fired as the Mexican fired again, fired as the Mexican stumbled forward, fired as the Mexican staggered and dropped to his knees and fell facedown with his arms spread. There were three more shots at that time, exactly three, because I can hear them every time I picture what took place; the shots coming from the ridge above us, from Early who was up there. I turned, aiming the Spencer almost straight up, but there was no sign of him. (There was no sign of him ever again that I know of.) When I turned back again, I saw Russell lying facedown between the ore-cart tracks. In the quiet that followed, all of us went down there.

Frank Braden had been shot twice in the chest; there was also the wound in his left thigh and a bullet crease across the shin of his left boot which had not touched him. Frank Braden was dead.

The Mexican had been hit in the chest twice and once in the stomach; plus the wound in his side that looked awful enough to have killed him. He lived another hour or so, but never told us his name, though he asked what Russell's was.

John Russell had been shot three times low in the back. We turned him over and saw he had been hit twice again, through the neck and chest. He was dead.

I was the one rode to Delgado's, running the horse most of the way, and ruining it, not intending to but not caring either. Delgado sent one of his boys to Sweetmary for the deputy. Delgado and I rode back to the San Pete in a wagon and got there in the dark of early morning. You could hear the crickets in the old buildings. Down in the open the McLaren girl and Henry Mendez and Dr. Favor and his wife were by a fire they'd kept going. Only Mrs. Favor had slept. Mendez had dug two graves.

Delgado and I sat with them and by the time it

started to get light the Sweetmary deputy, J. R. Lyons, arrived.

He looked at the bodies, Braden's and the Mexican's by the graves, Russell's in the wagon. Dig a hole for him too, J. R. Lyons said. What's the difference? He's dead. The McLaren girl said look all you want, but keep your opinions; we were taking Russell to Sweetmary for proper burial with a Mass and all and if Mr. J. R. Lyons didn't like it he didn't have to attend.

J. R. Lyons said of course he would. Once Dr. Favor and the stolen government money were handed over to a United States marshal.

(Which was done. Dr. Favor was tried in the District Court at Florence about a month later and sentenced to seven years in a Yuma prison. Mrs. Favor was not at the trial.)

John Russell was buried at Sweetmary. It was strange that neither the McLaren girl nor Henry Mendez nor I said much about him until after the funeral, and when we did talk found there wasn't much to be said.

You can look at something for a long time and not see it until it has moved or run off. That was how we had looked at Russell. Now, nobody questioned why he had walked down that slope. What we asked ourselves was why we ever thought he wouldn't.

Maybe he was showing off a little bit when he asked each of us if we wanted to walk down to the Favor woman, knowing nobody would but himself.

Maybe he let us think a lot of things about him that weren't true. But as Russell would say, that was up to us. He let people do or think what they wanted while he smoked a cigarette and thought it out calmly, without his feelings getting mixed up in it. Russell never changed the whole time, though I think everyone else did in some way. He did what he felt had to be done. Even if it meant dying. So maybe you don't have to understand him. You just know him.

"Take a good look at Russell. You will never see another one like him as long as you live." That first day, at Delgado's, Henry Mendez said it all.

Coming Soon
Another Elmore Leonard Classic Western

In **THE BOUNTY HUNTERS,**
a cavalryman turned Indian scout
rides in pursuit of an Apache renegade.
Filled with the extraordinary characters,
desperate odds and the spirit of wild frontiers
as only Elmore Leonard can evoke them,
this is western writing at its very best.

———◆———

"Elmore Leonard is an awfully good writer
of the sneaky sort; he is so good,
you don't notice what he's up to."
Washington Post Book World

Dave Flynn stretched his boots over the footrest and his body eased lower into the barber chair. It was hot beneath the striped cloth, but the long ride down from Fort Thomas had made him tired and he welcomed the comfort of the leather chair more than he minded the heat. In Contention it was hot wherever you went, even though it was nearly the end of October.

He turned his head, feeling the barber behind him, and frowned at the glare framed in the big window. John Willet moved to his side and he saw the barber's right ear bright red and almost transparent with the glare behind it. Beneath the green eyeshade, Willet's face sagged impassively. It was a large face, with an unmoving toothpick protruding from the corner of the slightly open mouth, the toothpick seeming unnaturally small.

John Willet put his hand under the young man's chin, raising the head firmly. "Let's see how we're doing," he said, then stepped back cocking his head and studied the hairline thoughtfully. He tapped comb against scissors then moved them in a flitting automatic gesture close to Flynn's ear.

"How's it going with you?"

"All right," Flynn answered drowsily. The heat was making him sleepy and it felt good not to move.

"You still guiding for the soldier boys?"

"On and off."

"I can think of better ways to make a living."

"Maybe I'll stay in the shade and take up barbering."

"You could do worse." Willet stepped back and studied the hairline again. "I heard you was doing some prospecting . . . down in the Madres."

"For about a year and a half."

"You're back to guiding, now?" And when Flynn nodded, Willet said, "Then I don't have to ask you if you found anything."

For a few minutes he moved the scissors deftly over the brown hair, saying nothing, until he finished trimming. Then he placed the implements on the shelf and studied a row of bottles there.

"Wet it down?"

"I suppose."

"You can use it," Willet said, shaking a green liquid into his hand. "That sun makes the flowers grow . . . but your hair isn't flowers."

"What about Apaches?" Flynn said.

"What about them?"

"They don't wear hats. They have better hair than anybody."

"Sun don't affect a man that was born in hell," Willet said, and began rubbing the tonic into Flynn's scalp.

Flynn closed his eyes again. Maybe that was it, he thought. He remembered the first Apache he had ever seen. That had been ten years ago.

D. A. Flynn, at twenty the youngest first lieutenant on frontier station, took his patrol out of Fort Lowell easterly toward the Catalinas; it was dawn of a muggy July day. Before ten they sighted the smoke. Before noon they found the burned wagon and the two dead men, and the third staked to the ground staring at the sun . . . because he could not close his eyes with the lids cut off. Nor could he speak with his tongue gone. He tried to tell them by writing in the sand, but the marks made little sense because he could not see what he was writing, and he died before he could make them plainer. But out of a mesquite clump only a dozen yards from the wagon, his men dragged an Apache who had been shot through both legs, and there was all the explanation that was needed. He could not speak English and none of the soldiers could speak Chiricahua Apache, so the sergeant dragged him back into the mesquite. There was the heavy report of a revolving pistol and the sergeant reappeared, smiling.

The hell with it, Flynn thought.

He felt the barber's fingers rubbing hard against his scalp. His eyes were still closed, but he could no longer see the man without the eyelids. He heard the barber say then, "You're starting to lose your hair up front."

Willet combed the hair, which was straighter than usual with the tonic, brushing it almost flat across the forehead, then began to trim Flynn's full cavalry-type mustache. The thinning hair and dragoon mustache made him appear older, yet there was a softness to the weather-tanned face. It was thin-lined and the bone structure was small. Dave Flynn was a month beyond his thirty-first birthday, but from fifteen feet he looked forty. That's what patrols in Apache country will do.

"Hang on," John Willet said, moving around the chair. "I see a couple of wild hairs." He took a finer comb from that shelf and turning back to Flynn he looked up to see the small, black-suited man enter the shop.

"Mr. Madora."

Flynn opened his eyes.

Standing the way he was, just inside the doorway with his thumbs hooked into vest pockets, Joe Madora could be mistaken for a dry-goods drummer. He was under average height and heavy, his black suit clinging tightly to a thick frame, and the derby placed evenly over his eyebrows might have been a size too small. His mustache and gray-streaked beard told that he was well into his fifties and probably too old to be much good with the pistol he wore high on his right hip. But Joe Madora had been underestimated before, many times, by Apaches as well as white men. Most of them were dead . . . while Joe was still chief of scouts at Fort Bowie.

He stood unmoving, staring at Dave Flynn, until finally Flynn said, "What's the matter with you?"

Madora's grizzled face was impassive. "I'm trying to figure out if you got on a fancy-braid charro rig under that barber cloth."

"It takes longer than a year and a half to go Mexican." Flynn nodded to the antlers mounted next to the door. "There's my coat right there."

Madora glanced at the faded tan coat. "You're about due for a new one."

"I'm not the dude you are."

"You bet your sweet tokus you're not."

Flynn smiled faintly, watching the man who had taught him everything he knew about the Apache. The comical-looking little man who could almost read sign in the air and better than half the time beat the Apache at his own game. He had learned well from Joe Madora, and after he had resigned his commission, it was Joe who had recommended him and saw that he got a job as a contract guide.

"I hear you're back for more," Madora said.

"You know of an easier way to make money?"

"Just two. Find gold or a rich woman."

"Well, I've given up on finding gold."

"And no woman 'ud have a slow-movin' son of a bitch like you, so you don't have a choice at that."

John Willet said, "Joe, let me trim your beard. Be done here in a minute."

Madora nodded and eased himself into the other barber chair. "Where's Irv?"

"Irv went up to Willcox to get something for his wife . . . coming in on the train."

"That's good," Madora grunted. "He's a worse barber than you are." He looked at Flynn then. "I heard about your new job. Taking that kid down into the Madres . . ." He stopped, seeing Flynn glance toward the barber. "John, you keep your ears plugged."

"I never did pay attention to what you had to say," Willet answered.

To Madora, Flynn said, "How did you find out?"

"I been guiding for Deneen. I heard him talking to this Bowers kid. Did he talk it over with you yet?"

"This morning for a minute. He kept reminding me I didn't have to take it, saying, 'You can back out,' using those words. Then he said, 'Think it over and come back later.' "

Madora smiled in his beard. "What about Bowers, did you see him?"

Flynn shook his head. He said then, "In the war we had a division commander by that name."

"Maybe he's a kin."

"What kind is he?"

"If you keep him from wettin' his pants he might do."

"How old?"

"Twenty-one . . . -two."

"West Point?"

"They all are . . . that doesn't mean anything. He's been out here a year and that's Whipple Barracks. He looks brevet-conscious. He wants to move up so bad he can taste it . . . and he's afraid going away on this job might get him lost in the woods."

"It could get him a promotion."

"It could get him killed, too. But he thinks it's more a job for a truant officer than a cavalryman. He said to Deneen, 'Sir, isn't bringing an old Indian back more a task for the reservation agent?' "

"Did you tell Bowers what it's all about?"

"He didn't ask me."

Flynn shook his head. "It doesn't make sense."

"You ought to be used to that; you've worked for Deneen before," Madora said. "His naming Bowers doesn't make sense . . . though he must have a reason. But it's plain why he's sending you."

"Why?"

"You know as well as I do. He wants to make

you quit again. You've done it twice before. Maybe he thinks one more will finish you for good."

"What do you think?" Flynn asked.

"I don't blame you for anything you did before. Deneen's Department Adjutant . . . with more weight than you got. When he says dance, you dance, or else go listen to a different tune. I wouldn't blame you too much if you backed out of this one. Only I think it can be done. I think you just might be able to drag Soldado Viejo—the old Indian, as the kid calls him—back to San Carlos."

"Two of us?"

"Two make less noise."

"Give me a better reason."

"Because I taught you what you know. And I'll give you one more," Madora added. "Because you might be mad enough to do this one just so you can throw it back in Deneen's face."

Flynn smiled. "You sound like you want to go."

"Maybe I should."

"Maybe you volunteered"—Flynn was still smiling—"but they said it wasn't something for an old man who looked like he was standing in a hole."

Madora shook his head. "I was wrong. You'll last down there about a day and a half."

"I've lasted ten years so far . . . plus three in the war when I didn't see you around."

"I was watchin' the frontier for you sword-clickin' bastards back East."

"About three thousand miles from Lee."

Madora was composed. "David," he said quietly. "All during that war of yours we had us a Mimbre named Soldado Viejo . . . the same one you're supposed to bring home. And I'll tell you something else. Bobby Lee, in his prime, couldn't rear-guard for Soldado if all the old Mimbre raided was whorehouses."

John Willet had looked from one to the other, trying to piece the conversation into some sense. Now he put down his comb and scissors and offered a hand mirror to Flynn.

"See how it looks," he said.

His gaze went to the window, idly, and he watched a man come out of the Republic House and start diagonally across the street toward the barbershop. Over the thick green lettering that read WILLET'S from the street side, he watched the man approach; long strides, but weaving somewhat, carrying a rifle in his right hand and saddlebags over his left shoulder. Then he recognized the man.

"God, I hope he hasn't been drinking."

Neither Flynn nor Madora had noticed him yet.

Willet spoke hurriedly, watching the man reach the plank sidewalk. "That's Frank Rellis . . . sometimes he acts funny when he's had a drink, but don't pay any attention to him."

Flynn, holding the mirror, glanced up. "What?"

But Willet was looking toward the door. "Hello, Frank . . . be with you in a minute."

Frank Rellis stood in the doorway swaying slightly, then came in and unslung the saddlebags, dropping them onto the seat of a Douglas chair next to the door. He eyed the occupied barber chairs sullenly; a man about Flynn's age, he wore range clothes: a sweat-stained hat, the curled brim close over his eyes, leather pants worn to a shine and a cotton shirt that was open enough to show thick dark hair covering his chest. His pistol was strapped low on his thigh and he still held the rifle, a Winchester, pointed toward the floor.

He looked at Willet. "Where's Irv?"

"Irv had to go to Willcox," John Willet said pleasantly. "I'll be with you in a minute . . . take a chair."

"I don't have a minute."

Willet smiled. "Frank, this being herd boss keeps you on the go, don't it?"

Rellis looked at the barber impassively. His deep-set eyes were half closed from drink and an apparent lack of sleep and a two days' beard stubble made his heavy-boned face menacing. "I said I don't have a minute."

Willet smiled, but now it was forced. "I'm finishing up, then I have to trim this here gent's beard"—he nodded to Joe Madora—"and I'll be with you."

"You can do better than that."

"Frank, I don't see any other way . . ."

"I do . . . you're taking me right now."

"Frank . . ."

"You can finish them up after."

Flynn glanced from Rellis to Madora. The chief of scouts was watching Rellis closely. "Are you in a hurry?" Madora said then.

Rellis ignored him, moving toward the first chair. He stopped at the footrest, in front of Flynn's boots. The mirror was still in his hand, but Flynn was looking over it at Rellis.

"You look prettier'n a French pimp," Rellis said. "Now get out of the chair."

Flynn felt the sudden flush of anger come over his face, but he took his time. His eyes left Rellis as he raised the mirror and studied his reflection, and he was surprised that his anger did not show. Perhaps the brown face had a reddish tint to it, but that was all. Then he said, quietly, "John, you're a little uneven right in through here"—his left hand following the part—"let's try parting it a little higher."

"Looks fine to me," Willet said uneasily. "That's the way you always wear it."

"I want to try all kinds of styles," Flynn said

evenly, "before I get old and set in my ways and have to live with it the rest of my life." He looked at Rellis, whose mouth had tightened. "I've got all afternoon. You can try parting it on the other side, then in the middle, then if you run out of ideas get your book out and look up a new one."

There was a silence and suddenly a brittle tension that was ready to break. Rellis' jaw tightened and colored a deeper red beneath the beard stubble. His body was stiff as if poised to make a move.

And then Joe Madora laughed. It was a soft chuckle, but it split the silence.

Rellis turned on him. "Are you laughing at me!" His face was beet-red now.

Madora's smile straightened and suddenly his dark face was cold and dead serious. He said to Rellis, "If you're not man then you shouldn't drink that lizard-pee they pass off as whisky over at the Republic."

Rellis didn't move. Flynn felt the tension and it made him ease up straighter in the chair. He looked at Rellis standing on the edge of his nerves gripping the Winchester tightly, cradled under his arm now. Rellis' eyes were wide with disbelief, staring at the little man with the beard . . . a head smaller than he was, older, and wearing his pistol in a high, awkward position. But Madora looked back at him calmly and something stopped Rellis at the peak of his anger.

"Mister," Flynn said now, and waited until Rellis looked at him. "You don't need a shave as bad as you think you do. Maybe you better get while your luck's still holding out."

Amazement was on Rellis' face, but he was near the end of his patience and the anger was plain on his face. "What's your name?" he said.

"Flynn."

"We ever met before?"

"I doubt it."

"Are you going to get out of that chair, or do I pry you out with this?" He raised the Winchester slightly.

"You raise that another inch," Flynn said calmly, "I'll kill you."

Rellis stopped. He looked at the long barber cloth that covered Flynn to the knees, smooth striped cotton that told nothing.

"You're bluffing."

"There's one way to find out."

Rellis glanced quickly at the antlers next to the door. A tan coat hung there; a gun belt could be beneath it, but it could also be in Flynn's hand beneath the cloth.

John Willet's face turned paler under the eye shade. He said, his voice faltering, "Gentlemen, please . . ." But that was all.

Rellis moved suddenly toward the chair, but Flynn's boot kicked out in the same motion and caught him in the pit of the stomach. Rellis went back with a rip up his shirt front where Flynn's spur had slashed, and as he staggered back, Flynn came out of the chair and swung the hand mirror hard against the side of Rellis' head while his right hand wrenched at the Winchester.

The rifle barrel swung back toward Rellis, even while his hand was still on the stock, and came down across his skull. He didn't go down, but staggered backward with Flynn pushing him toward the open door, and in the doorway Flynn stopped, holding the rifle, while Rellis kept going, stumbling, until he landed in the dust on his back and rolled over. He was raising himself to his knees when his saddlebags came flying out to catch him full in the face and knock him flat again.

Flynn turned back into the shop and placed the rifle against the wall below the antlers. "Give him his rifle back when he gets some sense," he said to John Willet.

Joe Madora came out of the chair. "Some other time, John. You look a mite too nervous to be wielding scissors." He nodded to the broken glass from the hand mirror. "David, you just acquired seven years of the worst kind of luck."

Flynn paid Willet, who took the money silently, then moved to the antlers. He took down his coat, then lifted off his gun harness and passed his arm through the sling so that the holster hung well below his left armpit, the long-barreled .44 extending past his belt. He put on the tan coat, faded, bleached almost white. His light Stetson was sweat-stained around the band and he wore the stiff brim straight, close over his eyes. Putting it on, he said, "We'll see you again, John."

Willet said now, "He's not going to forget that. Dave, you don't know that man."

Madora said, "But he knows Dave now."